Evan
Help Us

Also by Rhys Bowen

Evans Above

Evan Help Us

Rhys Bowen

ST. MARTIN'S PRESS ❦ NEW YORK

Production Editor: David Stanford Burr

ISBN 0-312-19411-0

This book is dedicated to the memory of my mother, Margery Lee (née Rees). Her passing has left a dark void in my life. I'll miss her love, her companionship, and, above all, her laughter.

The Legend of Beddgelert

Prince Llewellyn had a faithful dog called Gelert. One day he went out hunting, leaving his dog to guard his young son. On his return he found the baby's cradle empty and the dog covered in blood. In rage and despair he took out his sword and struck down Gelert. It was only as the dog lay dying that Llewellyn noticed the carcass of a huge wolf lying on the floor and the little prince, safely asleep in the corner. He ran to Gelert, but it was too late. The dog died in his arms.

In the dog's honor he erected an impressive tomb, which can be seen today in the village that bears the name of Beddgelert—Gelert's Grave.

This dramatic legend is now thought to have been created by an enterprising nineteenth-century innkeeper. Scholars now think that the name referred to an early saint, not Llewellyn's dog.

Chapter 1

Colonel Arbuthnot strode out over the springy turf, his cheeks puffed out as trombone-like sounds popped from his pursed lips. The music was just recognizable as "Men of Harlech." Sheep glanced up from their grazing and scattered, alarmed at the strange sounds coming from the colonel's lips, and at the rhythmic thwacking of his silver-tipped cane against clumps of gorse and bracken.

Although he was approaching eighty, the colonel was an imposing figure, with an upright bearing and a purposeful stride. He had been a handsome man in his day and still liked to think that the ladies found him attractive. He sported a neat little moustache, but heavy jowls now sagged on either side of it and his once fearsome eyebrows stuck out like prawns over faded watery eyes. Even though it was midsummer, the colonel wore his habitual tweed jacket with a canary yellow waistcoat beneath it, a checked shirt, and a silk paisley cravat around his neck. His only concession to the season was a faded panama straw hat which he wore whenever possible to keep the sun off his bald spot. The village children of Llanfair imitated the colonel's distinctive gait, but never to his face.

A stiff mountain breeze blew in Colonel Arbuthnot's face. He paused and breathed deeply.

"Ah," he said, thumping his chest. "That's more like it."

He felt alive for the first time in months. God, it was good to get away from that dreary London flat. All those interminable days of silence, broken only by brisk walks to the library to read newspapers he could no longer afford to buy, or, on fine days, a constitutional twice around the pond in the park. Fortunately he had bought a life membership to his club in his more affluent days, but he hardly ever went there any more. There seemed little point in it since old Chaterham had died last year. He was now the only one of his generation left and the young fellows weren't interested in what he had to say. They thought he was an old codger and made excuses to hurry off somewhere—always in a hurry, the younger generation seemed to be. Constantly at the mercy of those damned portable phones. No time to enjoy life. Colonel Arbuthnot pitied them. At least he'd known the good life once. He'd been on tiger shoots and dined with maharajahs and made love to pretty women in marble palaces. The young knew nothing about sport or conversation or romance. No manners and no time, the colonel decided, savagely decapitating a large thistle.

Clouds raced overhead, opening up brief tantalizing vistas of mountains, lakes and steep meadows dotted with sheep. He hadn't realized how high he had climbed. Not bad for a senior citizen, he told himself. He'd wager those young weaklings at the club couldn't keep up with him, for all the time they claimed to spend keeping fit at their health clubs.

Below him the village of Llanfair lay like a row of doll houses, bordering the road as it climbed the pass and skirted around Mount Snowdon. The colonel looked down at it fondly. With its plain, slate-roofed cottages, it could hardly compare in beauty to one of the quaint, cozy English villages with their thatched roofs and cottage gardens. But its setting, high on the pass with peaks soaring on either side, was spectacular.

At the far end of the village he picked out the larger shape of the Red Dragon pub, its painted sign swinging in front. Just how a pub should be, he told himself, as he nodded in satisfaction. Always enough chaps around with time for a chat, women usually confined to the lounge where they could be seen and not heard; just how he liked things to be. Lovely creatures, women, but inclined to babble on meaninglessly unless curbed—except for Joanie. She had never babbled. She'd listen to his stories with a gentle smile on her lips and always laughed at his jokes. God, he still missed her so much . . .

At least they were polite enough to listen to his stories at the pub here in Llanfair. They even pretended to be interested. "So, did you ever shoot a tiger, colonel?" they'd ask and he'd be able to answer, "Shoot a tiger? I can tell you about the time I bagged three tigers in one day. We had to pretend that the maharajah had shot them, of course. Protocol demanded it. But it was really my bullet each time that finished them off. One was a great brute eight feet long. I've got a picture of it on my mantelpiece at home . . ."

The colonel smiled in anticipation of being asked to tell that story again. They were good chaps here in Llanfair—simple Welsh villagers of course, but they made him feel welcome. He knew this was quite different from the way they treated most foreigners. He'd watched them switch into Welsh in midconversation when tourists walked in. But he supposed that his Welsh wife had made him somehow acceptable.

He remembered the first time Joanie had taken him to Wales when they were home on leave together. He hadn't realized until then that Wales was a foreign country. Hearing her chatting in a language he couldn't understand had amazed and impressed him—it was a side of her he had never suspected. Thinking of Joanie now brought back the leaden feeling to his heart. It was amazing that one could miss a person for so long.

3

She had been dead for ten years and he still felt it as if it was yesterday.

He had come to Wales the summer after Joanie's death, trying to make sense of things, and had been healed and charmed by the silent, rugged beauty of the mountains of Snowdonia. By sheer luck he had seen an advertisement for summer accommodation at Owens' farm above Llanfair. His gaze moved beyond the village to the square whitewashed farmhouse, protected by a stand of windswept trees. Answering that advertisement had been one of the luckiest things he'd ever done, and he'd certainly had lucky moments in his life— like the time a charging rhino had run right past him or when Charlotte's husband had shot at him and missed as he leaped from the houseboat window into the lake at Kashmir.

Mrs. Owens spoiled him shamelessly, making his favorite meals and encouraging him to have seconds and thirds of everything his doctor had strictly forbidden. She did his washing and ironing and kept his room spotless without fussing over him. His days were free to be spent in the good fresh air, tramping over the hills, trying to identify wild flowers or birds, or pursuing his real passion, archaeology. He'd been a keen amateur archaeologist from the age of eight when he uncovered a Roman coin in a field near his home in Yorkshire. He had been awestruck that objects two thousand years old were lying at his feet, waiting to be rediscovered. If he'd come from a different family, he might have gone to Oxford or Cambridge to study ancient history, but the Arbuthnots always went into the army. He sighed.

His passion for archaeology was one of the reasons that drew him back to Wales. He wanted to be the one to prove, beyond a doubt, that King Arthur had actually existed. There were enough local legends to support it, of course. Up on Mount Snowdon there was the Bwlch y Saethau (the Pass of Arrows) where Arthur was mortally wounded while about to defeat Mordred. Excalibur was said to have appeared from Llyn

Llydaw, the lake that nestled on the flanks of Snowdon. He could see it now, glistening in bright sunlight. Even the peak of Snowdon itself was called Yr Wyddfa, meaning burial site, by the locals. Only a great king would have been buried on the highest mountain peak in Wales. If only he could find something definitive to prove Arthur's existence. That was what kept him going these days.

He sat on an outcropping of rock and took out his binoculars. There had once been a Bronze Age fort guarding the pass. If he could find evidence of that, it would be a good start.

His gaze swept from the summit of Snowdon, across the other peaks whose names he had forgotten, and down to the village again. They were good binoculars, made in Germany back in the old days when things were built to last. He picked out a figure sitting on the humped stone bridge that spanned the noisy little mountain stream. It must be that idiot postman, he decided—the one they called Evans-the-Post. He always sat and read the mail before he delivered it. Funny how nobody seemed to mind . . . His gaze moved up the street. He saw the young policeman making his afternoon rounds. He liked Constable Evans—good-looking young chap, sturdily built like a rugby player, not like some of the effeminate young men these days with their dreadful earrings. Colonel Arbuthnot had often consulted him about the best hiking trails or the identity of a certain bird or flower. Of course the young fellow had landed himself an easy job, running a police substation in a village like Llanfair. Hardly a hotbed of crime, the colonel decided, taking in the empty street and the children playing in the school yard.

He adjusted his focus, hoping to get a glimpse of the schoolteacher. A pretty young filly, slim and graceful. She reminded him of Joanie when they had first met at that garden party in Delhi. He heard the faint ringing of a bell and the children immediately formed two lines and began to file back into the building.

The colonel's gaze moved on. The last two buildings in the village were both chapels, one on either side of the street. He'd never been able to understand why a village the size of Llanfair needed two places of worship—but of course the Welsh did love their religion. They sat through interminable sermons and sang hymns on any excuse. Fine singing too, not the half-hearted muttering of the All Saints Church parishioners at home in Kensington.

The binoculars swept idly over the village again and then the colonel stiffened, blinking his eyes to bring one figure into focus. "Extraordinary!" the colonel said out loud. "It can't be." Someone was standing in the middle of the village street, looking around with interest. It almost seemed to the colonel that their eyes met, although he knew that was impossible. But he felt the keen gaze lingering in the direction of the rock where he now sat. Then the person turned and disappeared into the shadow between two cottages.

The colonel let out a sigh and shook his head. His eyesight must be failing him in his old age. He had just seen someone who couldn't possibly be here. It was absurd. His eyes were playing tricks on him.

He lowered the binoculars and sat staring out into space. Of course he was mistaken, he told himself. Everyone in the world had a double, hadn't they? He got up and brushed off his trousers. Dashed awkward if it really had been who he'd imagined, he told himself. Dashed awkward for both of them, he suspected.

Then something happened to drive everything else from his mind. He found himself staring at the rocks where he had just been sitting. They were covered in gorse and bracken, but there was a certain evenness and regularity about them. As he looked more closely, he could see that they formed a perfect rectangle enclosing a grassy area. Excitedly he pulled at the gorse, oblivious to scratches, and found himself staring at what was definitely an old wall. He scrambled over and started to clear away grass and weeds. Yes, here was the entrance, and just inside what looked like a smooth stone slab! The colonel dropped to his knees and began to pull away weeds, oblivious to anything and anyone around him . . .

Chapter 2

Constable Evan Evans of the North Wales police walked slowly up the main street of Llanfair. To be more accurate, it was the only street in Llanfair, apart from some muddy tracks that led to a couple of farmhouses. Like many Welsh villages it had been built in the heyday of the slate quarries. It was an unpretentious little place—two rows of stone cottages, a few shops, a petrol pump, and a couple of chapels lining the road that climbed the pass to the foot of Mount Snowdon. It could be bleak and windy at times, when cloud and snow blanketed the peaks above, but its spectacular setting made up for the lack of architectural wonders.

Constable Evans paused on the old stone bridge that spanned the rushing mountain stream and looked around him with satisfaction. Llanfair might not be the most beautiful nor the most exciting place on earth, but it was alright with him. He took in the clear water dancing over mossy rocks and traced it upward to the bright ribbon of water that fell from the sheer mountainside. On the breeze he caught the faint bleating of sheep. It was the only sound, apart from the splash and gurgle of the water and the sigh of wind through the alder trees along the stream.

8

Evan glanced up the street. There was no traffic, which was unusual for a sunny summer afternoon, although it was getting late. Most tourists would already be back at their hotels or bed-and-breakfasts, debating whether they'd be able to find Mexican food or pizza in a primitive place like Wales.

Even though it was almost six o'clock, the sun was still high in the sky. This far north it wouldn't set until after nine. The long light evenings were one of the bonuses of living in North Wales. He stood there, breathing deeply, at peace with the world.

He heard the sound of running feet on the road behind him and turned to watch a group of village boys, dressed in football uniforms, run past.

" 'Ello, Mr. Efans! Sut yrch chi?" they called out in their high, musical voices, using the mixture of Welsh and English that they usually spoke.

"Hello, boys. Off to football practice are you then?" Evan called back.

They nodded, their faces alight with anticipation. "We're playing down in Beddgelert on Saturday—big match of the year!" one of them said.

"They beat us last year, but we're going to show them this time," another added.

"Are you coming to watch, Mr. Efans?" the first boy asked. "It's going to be good. We've got Ivor on our team now, and he's ever so fast. He won the hundred yards dash on sports day."

"I'll be there if I can," Evan called after them as they ran on up the street toward the school playground. He smiled as he watched them go, remembering himself at their age—undersized, skinny, all legs like them.

A village constable—or a community police presence as they called it now—was the best kind of policeman to be, he thought. It was amazing to be paid for what he liked doing most, walking around and talking to people.

A few years ago there had been a national movement to modernize and streamline the police force. They had closed all the substations and covered the area with car patrols from HQ. But they'd soon realized their mistake. A police presence in the villages, a local bobby who knew everyone and their business, was the biggest deterrent to crime. So local substations and community police teams were opening again all over the country.

Evan had read about this move just over a year ago, when he was recovering from the trauma of his father's death. They had been working the tough dockland beat in Swansea together when his father caught a bullet during a drug bust. Afterward he no longer wanted to be part of a force that threw away good lives so meaninglessly.

Now he was glad he had decided to take this job instead of quitting the police force. He had never regretted coming here. He liked the locals. They liked him. The pace was slow and the mountains were waiting to be climbed whenever he had free time.

He gazed up at the peaks. Snowdon was glowing with that pink light of early evening. Evan glanced at his watch . . . maybe there would be time for a quick scramble up to Bwlch y Moch after he had closed up and changed out of his uniform—if he could slip in and out of the house without his landlady hearing.

He had been lodging with Mrs. Williams ever since he came to Llanfair and mostly he was content. She was a kind, motherly woman but she had two faults: She was determined to fatten him up like a prize turkey by feeding him three enormous meals a day, and she was equally determined to get him married off to her granddaughter Sharon, who was herself built with the girth of a prize turkey.

Evan sighed and walked on up the street, past a row of shops on the right. G. Evans, butcher, was next to R. Evans, dairy products. The monopoly was spoiled by T. Harris, gen-

10

eral store and post office. As Evan passed, the door of the first shop was flung open and a big man in a blood-spattered apron leaped out, waving a murderous-looking meat cleaver.

"Nos da, good evening, Evans-the-Law," he called out. "Solved any juicy murders today then?" He laughed loudly at his own joke.

"Not yet, Evans-the-Meat," Evan called back. "But there's still time, isn't there? Are you planning on committing one?"

"I just might," Evans-the-Meat replied, the smile fading from his face. "I'd like to murder all those bloody tourists. Why can't they leave us alone, that's what I want to know."

Evan looked up and down the deserted street. Even in the height of the summer holidays, Llanfair could hardly be described as a tourist mecca. There was little here to make them stop—a petrol pump with small snack bar, and postcards that were sold at the post office and general store. A couple of cottages took in b-and-b visitors, and four new holiday bungalows had appeared this spring on Morgan's farm, but that was the extent of the hospitality industry in the village itself. The well-heeled drivers of BMWs and Jags stayed at the new Everest Inn, further up the pass. Evan glanced up at the overgrown Swiss chalet that had so enraged the residents when it was built. It still looked monstrously out of place—a kind of Disney mountain fantasy on a bleak Welsh hillside.

"It's not like we're overrun with tourists here, is it?" Evan voiced his thoughts out loud. "And Roberts-the-Pump likes the extra money he gets selling snacks."

Evans-the-Meat sniffed in disgust. "Sell his own mother for tuppence, that man would," he said. "And that idiot Evans-the-Milk too." He added this loudly, glancing hopefully at the open door of the dairy. One of his main hobbies was fighting with his next-door neighbor. But nobody came out of the dairy to meet the challenge.

"Evans-the-Milk?" Evans asked. "What's he selling then?"

Evans-the-Meat leaned closer as if he was divulging a great

secret. "He's planning to make his own ice cream, that's what," he hissed. "He thinks the tourists will come running. I told him I didn't want to see another tourist anywhere near my shop!"

Evan grinned. "But the tourists don't bother you, do they?"

He couldn't imagine too many out-of-town visitors would find a reason to pop into a butcher's shop.

"Those people staying at the new holiday bungalows do," Evans-the-Meat said. He glanced up at four new wood and glass structures that stood on what used to be Taff Morgan's farm. They had been built during the spring and the villagers complained that Taff's son Ted hadn't even waited until his poor father was cold in his grave before he started spoiling things with his fancy London ways. Not that he ever came near the place himself. A contractor had simply shown up one day with instructions to build, and Mr. Ted Morgan hadn't even come to check on the result.

Evans-the-Meat came closer, still waving his cleaver. "Would you like to hear what happened today, then?" he asked confidentially. "One of those English people from the bungalows had the nerve to ask me if I had any decent English lamb! I told her the day I had to start selling foreign lamb was the day I closed my doors for good."

Evan tried not to smile. "I don't suppose she's ever had the opportunity to try our local Welsh lamb," he said easily.

"Then it's about time she bloody learned, isn't it?" Evans-the-Meat snapped. He headed back to his store, then turned to Evan again.

"See you at the Dragon then, will I?"

Evan nodded. "I expect so. As soon as I've closed up shop at the police station."

"It must be hard, all that walking up and down and stopping for cups of tea," Evans-the-Meat said.

Evan smiled, although he was never quite sure when Evans-the-Meat was joking.

"It's a tough job, but someone's got to do it, haven't they?" he retorted. "See you then. Don't go waving that thing around, will you, or I might have to cite you for carrying a deadly weapon." He gave a friendly wave to the butcher and headed on up the street.

The boys were already in the midst of their football practice when he reached the village school. He paused to watch for a moment, his gaze straying to the gray stone school building beyond. Bronwen often stayed late to prepare the next day's lessons. He hoped she'd glimpse him outside and come out to talk. Evan wasn't usually shy about talking to women, but he had been deliberately taking it slowly with Bronwen Price. Sometimes he wondered if she wasn't a little too serious and intellectual for him. He knew very well that two dates with one girl in a village like Llanfair would have everyone planning the wedding day. It wasn't that he didn't want to get married some day, but he wasn't in any big hurry either.

But he certainly enjoyed Bronwen's company and her quiet wisdom. She was the one person he could talk to when he had something on his mind. She was a great listener and didn't make any rash judgements. The way she sat there, her head slightly on one side, her long ash blond hair falling like a curtain of golden rain, had often encouraged him to say far more than he had meant to. And he had gone away feeling strangely content.

But Bronwen didn't appear from the school today and Evan resumed his trek to the top of the village street. The last two buildings were both chapels. On the left was Chapel Bethel, Reverend Parry Davies, Sunday school 10 A.M. worship service 6 P.M. (sermon in English). On the right was Chapel Beulah, Reverend Powell-Jones, worship service 6 P.M. (sermon in Welsh and English). They framed the street, unpretentious gray stone mirror images of each other, even to the identical billboards beside their front doors. Only the biblical texts on their billboards were different.

13

If the outsider paused to wonder why a village the size of Llanfair needed two chapels, the messages on the billboards should have given him a clue. The two chapels were at constant war. Today the message outside Chapel Bethel read "Vengeance is mine, says the Lord," while Beulah proclaimed, "Forgive your enemies. Turn the other cheek!"

Evan grinned. The war of the billboards was the civilized way that Reverends Parry Davies and Powell-Jones got at each other. When one came out with a new billboard quote, the other rushed straight to his Bible to contradict or better it. There was no animosity more passionate than that between rival Christians, Even thought.

He had reached the end of the village. Before him the road snaked up to the top of the pass, a gray ribbon between green hills. The only building was the Everest Inn, its wood-shingled Swiss chalet roof glowing in the evening sunlight. Evan paused and scanned the hills above. He picked out a figure moving across the high pastures and caught the glint of something bright. That would be the colonel's silver-tipped cane, he decided. On his way down from another of his expeditions. He marvelled at the old man's strength and determination. He must be going on eighty and yet he was up there, tramping around, wet or dry, determined to come up with King Arthur's crown, or maybe the rotting remains of the round table.

As Evan turned to head back to the police station, his attention was caught by something lower down the mountain. There was a flash of bright red in the meadow behind Chapel Bethel. It was a little girl with red-blond curls and a bright red dress. She was skipping across the grass so lightly that she looked weightless. Evan didn't recognize her as one of the village kids. She must be an outsider, staying at the holiday cottages, and rather young to be out alone, even in a safe place like Llanfair, he thought.

He scanned the road for signs of someone keeping an eye on her, saw no one, and decided to keep an eye on her himself.

14

It was an awfully big mountain up there and he didn't want her to stray too far. Then she stopped her upward trek and started to come back. Evan sighed in relief. She was almost back to the dry-stone wall when she broke into a run. Evan saw she was heading for a young lamb, standing alone not far from the wall. He heard her call to it and throw open her arms as if she expected it to come to her like a puppy. Strangely enough the lamb didn't run away. The little girl put her arms around it and picked it up. It was heavier than she had expected and she staggered forward with it, her face red with exertion. Evan wondered what she intended to do with it and where she was trying to take it.

But he never found out because the lamb started struggling and bleating frantically. Its cries reached the ears of its mother, grazing not too far away. The old sheep raised her head and then came waddling to the defence of her offspring. The little girl looked around to see a large sheep charging toward her, uttering threatening baas. She dropped the lamb and fled back to the wall, as fast as her little legs could carry her.

Evan ran to meet her, in case she needed help getting over the wall. But she scrambled over and jumped down the other side, her eyes still wide with fear. She ran down the bank, gathering speed as she went, and shot straight out into the road. Subconsciously Evan's ears had picked up the whine of an approaching car some time ago. The whine had now become a roar. The little girl heard it too and froze in the middle of the road as the car came speeding up the pass.

Evan rushed out into the road, snatched her up, and flung her to one side as the car swerved, breaks squealing and horn blaring. It passed them within inches and screeched to a halt.

"Phew, that was a close one," the driver yelled, his face a sickly green.

"No harm done luckily," Evan called back. He waved to the driver as the car took off again. "It's alright, love. You're fine." He smiled down at the child who had started to cry.

A scream made him look up. A young woman was running across the street, her eyes wide with terror. Her hair was a darker shade of red than the girl's, but she was unmistakably her mother.

"Jenny! Ohmygod, Jenny! What happened? Is she all right?" she shrieked.

Evan set the little girl down. "She's fine. Had a bit of a scare, didn't you, love?" he asked the little girl. He didn't add that he'd had a bit of a scare too. He could feel his heart still thumping.

"The bear chased me," Jenny said, rushing to cling to her mother's legs. "It growled at me."

"Bear?" The mother looked at Even for explanation.

"She means sheep," Evan said. "She picked up a lamb and its mother came after her."

The young woman looked apologetically at Evan as she enfolded the child in her arms. "We're from Manchester. She's never seen a sheep before."

The little girl sobbed against her mother's shoulder, her thin body heaving with each sob. The woman held her more tightly. "You were a bad girl to go out without Mummy, weren't you?"

The little girl nodded, her lower lip trembling.

"It's my fault, I suppose," the woman said, straightening up again. Evan was interested to hear that her accent sounded more London than Manchester. "It was such a lovely day that I had the doors open. She must have gone out the front door while I was busy cooking her tea." She glanced across to the row of cottages opposite, where one front door stood wide open. "I didn't think too much could happen in a place like this if you left the doors and windows open," she added.

"There are still cars on the street," Evan said. "You can never be too careful with kids, can you?"

"You're right there." She shook her head, giving him an exasperated smile. "She's a little monkey, she is. Into every-

16

thing the moment my back's turned, aren't you, you horrible little monster?" She nuzzled at the child's neck, making the little girl stop crying and squeal with delight.

Now that the trauma was over, Evan noticed that she was a good-looking young woman, although her bright red hair, plucked and pencilled eyebrows, and heavy makeup seemed out of place in Llanfair, as were the skimpy white shorts and Hawaiian print halter top she was wearing. Not that they didn't suit her with those long legs . . .

Evan forced his mind back to business. "Here for a holiday, are you?"

The young woman looked up, the little girl still clinging to her neck. "No, we just moved here a couple of days ago."

"Moved here? For good, you mean?" Evan was surprised. Usually the village grapevine would have found out the moment anyone new arrived. This one seemed to have slipped in unnoticed.

"I can't say how good it will be yet." The woman smiled again. There was a wistful quality to her smile. "I thought we'd give it a try here. I wanted her to grow up somewhere healthy and safe, away from all the drugs and crime."

"But why here?" Evan asked. "You're not Welsh, are you?"

She chuckled. "If you heard me trying to say Chlanfair, you'd know the answer to that one. No, I've no connections with the place, which is part of the attraction, I suppose."

"Then why here? Had you been here on holiday when you were a kid?"

She paused for a moment, staring out past him to the green hillsides. Evan wondered if he was being too inquisitive. "I'm sorry, I'm giving you the third degree," he said. "I'll leave you to get back to your tea."

"I don't really know what made me come here myself," she said as he started to move away. "I'd never even seen the place before—not in the flesh anyway. I'd, uh, heard about it and it just seemed like a good place to bring up a kid."

17

"So what do you think about it now that you're here?" Evan asked.

She glanced up and down the street. A couple of men were walking past on their way to the pub, hands in their pockets and their caps pulled down over their eyes. A woman came out of her cottage further down the row and yelled back a torrent of Welsh insults as she left.

The young woman turned back to Evan. "I didn't expect it to be so . . . foreign. There's no way I'll ever learn to talk Welsh. I suppose I'll always be an outsider."

"Give them time," Evan said. "They're friendly enough, once they get used to you. It's just that we Welsh are a little shy and suspicious around strangers."

"You don't seem too shy." The woman gave him a challenging smile.

"Ah well, it's my job, isn't it?" Evan could feel himself flushing and cursed his fair Celtic skin that showed the least embarrassment.

"So you're the local bobby, are you?"

Evan nodded. "Constable Evans. I run the community police station here."

She managed to free one arm while the little girl still clung to her and extended her hand to him. "Pleased to meet you, Constable Evans. I'm Annie. Annie Pigeon."

"Nice to meet you, Annie." Evan took her hand. "Welcome to Llanfair. If you need any help, just come to me." He gave her a friendly smile. "I'd better get going. I've got to report in to HQ before I close up shop for the night. See you around then, Annie, and you too, Jenny. No more running out into the street without your mum, okay?"

The little girl glanced at him shyly then buried her head in her mother's shoulder.

"She's kind of shy around strangers, just like you Welsh people," Annie said, her eyes challenging again. "I'd best be getting back to my cooking, if you can call baked beans and frankfurters cooking. See you then, constable, or do you have a first name?"

"It's Evan."

"Evan Evans?" She let out a shriek of laughter. "That's about as bloody Welsh as you can get, isn't it?"

Evan started to walk away as she made for her front door.

"Bye, Evan," she called after him. "See you around. Go on, Jenny, say good-bye."

He turned back, but Jenny's face was still buried. He continued down the street, intrigued by Annie Pigeon who just appeared spontaneously in a place she had never seen before. Why? Why would a big-city girl from England come to live in a remote village in Wales? He got the feeling that there was no Mr. Pigeon around, probably never had been. It wasn't going to be easy for a single mum, that was for sure. There was no denying that the Welsh took a long time to warm to strangers and most people in Llanfair spoke Welsh rather than English. He'd have to do what he could—

He stopped abruptly as he sensed, rather than saw, someone watching him. Bronwen Price was leaning on the gate to the school playground. Her ash blond braid hung over one shoulder, and the wind was blowing stray wisps of hair across her face. She was wearing a long blue cotton skirt and a blue denim shirt that matched her eyes.

"Good evening, Evan," she said, repeating his name exactly as Annie had called out after him.

Chapter 3

"Damn," Evan muttered under his breath.

He gave her a smile as he strolled over to her. "Oh, hullo there, Bronwen. You're working late tonight, aren't you?"

"I could say the same for you," Bronwen said, her gaze going past him up the street to a front door that was just closing. "Giving the tourists advice on the local attractions, were you?"

Evan couldn't tell from her voice whether she was annoyed or amused. "She's not a tourist. She's just moved here. Came from Manchester, of all places, and never been out of the city before by the sound of it. The little girl thought a sheep was a bear." He attempted to laugh but Bronwen was still looking at him with large, solemn eyes. She said nothing so he went on. "I imagine it won't be easy for her, coming here and not speaking Welsh."

"So you're going to help her get settled in."

"I think we all should help her," Evan said. "It can't be easy, alone with a little kid."

"You know your trouble, Evan Evans," Bronwen said.

"You're just an overgrown boy scout. You can't stop helping people, can you?"

"Just doing my job, Bronwen."

"Right," she said, giving him a sweet smile. "You'd better go and close up the station then, hadn't you? They'll be wondering down in Caernarfon where you've got to."

She turned away from the gate and Evan walked on, feeling annoyed and confused. Had she just been teasing him or did she really think he'd been unnecessarily attentive to Annie Pigeon? Why was it so damned hard to understand women? And why should it matter what she thought? It wasn't as if they were engaged or even officially dating. And yet Evan knew that it did matter. He cared more about Bronwen than he dared admit to himself. He liked having her around. He had come to rely on her. Like Henry Higgins, he had grown accustomed to her face. And he was approaching thirty—an age when a man should start to think about settling down.

It was almost seven when Evan finally headed home. He had sat at his desk, thinking, and his end-of-the-week paperwork had taken him twice as long as usual.

"Aren't you coming for a drink then, Evan bach?" Charlie Hopkins had called out to him as he passed him in the street. "It's Friday night, isn't it?"

"I'll be there," Evan called back. "I've got to go home and change first. Not allowed to drink in uniform, you know—bad for the image of the police force."

Mrs. Williams' house was on what was considered the superior side of the street. Rather than a row of cottages all joined together, the houses opposite the petrol station were built in three semidetached pairs. They were also simple gray stone buildings, hardly more than cottages themselves, but they were considered the upscale part of Llanfair by virtue of having what Mrs. Williams called a back parlor and a front parlor, neither

21

used except on special occasions, also what Mrs. Williams grandly referred to as her front garden—in reality a four-foot square of earth with a couple of sad roses growing in it.

"Is that you, Mr. Evans?" Mrs. Williams' voice sang out down the dark hallway as he attempted to close the front door silently behind him. He often wondered why the police force didn't hire Mrs. Williams as a local radar unit. She had an incredible sixth sense that alerted her to his key in the front door, even if the TV was blaring away or she was shut in the kitchen at the back of the house. It was impossible to enter or leave unnoticed, although Evan still tried.

"No, Mrs. Williams. It's a burglar," Evan called back, "who just happens to have a front door key."

Mrs. Williams' face, red and beaded with sweat from cooking, appeared at the open kitchen door. "Don't say things like that, Mr. Evans. You know I'm scared to death about burglars. It was the happiest day of my life when a policeman moved into my house. And you know what my daughter said? She said they'll think twice about breaking in now, now that I've got a big strong man like you in the house. She thinks very highly of you, my daughter does. So does my granddaughter, of course. We all do." She came down the hall to meet him and took his arm. "Come and sit you down now. Your dinner is all ready and waiting."

"I think I'll wait a while to eat, if you don't mind, Mrs. Williams," Evan said warily. "I told a couple of the lads that I'd meet them down at the Dragon. It is Friday night, after all."

"But I've made you a lamb cawl," she said, referring to the local thick Welsh lamb stew. "Your favorite." Everything she made was apparently Evan's favorite. "I got a lovely shoulder of lamb from Evans-the-Meat. And speaking of him," she went on, "did you hear that one of those English women staying up at Morgan's farm had the nerve to ask him why he didn't stock any English lamb? The nerve of it. Evans-the-Meat has never sold foreign meat in his life!"

22

Silently Evans complimented the efficiency of the village grapevine, then he remembered his encounter. "Did you hear that we've got new people living up next to Charlie Hopkins?" he asked.

"New people? Renting old Mrs. Hughes' cottage?" Mrs. Williams looked astonished.

"Moved in a couple of days ago," Evan said, delighted to be able to score a point for once. "A mother and her little girl."

"Well, I never," Mrs. Williams said. "And we heard nothing about it, did we? But then I think it was let through that fancy estate agent down in Caernarfon. Are they here for the summer?"

"For good, maybe," Evan said.

"And the husband will be joining them, no doubt?"

"I'm not sure about that," Evan said tactfully.

Mrs. Williams sniffed. "Just watch she doesn't try to get her claws into you," she said. "A good-looking young chap like yourself and at the right age to settle down too. You want to find yourself a nice local girl, one that knows how to cook and look after you properly." She broke off as if a thought had just struck her. "Now what does that remind me of?" She put her hand up to her mouth then a broad smile spread across her face. "Oh, by the way, did I tell you that our Sharon is taking one of these continental cooking classes at evening school? Last week it was spaghetti bolognese and this week it's some kind of French fish stew—booly base, I think she called it. She's a lovely little cook now and she'll be coming to visit as usual tomorrow."

Evan smiled politely. He hadn't ever had the heart to tell Mrs. Williams that her granddaughter Sharon was built like a rugby fullback and had the most annoying habit of giggling like a teenager at everything he said. As Bronwen had told him, one of his problems was that he hated to hurt people's feelings. Maybe he should start working on that right now.

"I'll just get changed and pop down to the Dragon, Mrs. Williams," he said. "Why don't you put my lamb cawl into the oven. I'll eat it when I get back."

"Just as you like, Mr. Evans." Mrs. Williams had a hurt look on her face but she gave up without a fight and went back into the kitchen. Evan felt that he had won a small victory as he climbed the stairs to change out of his uniform.

The Red Dragon was already in full Friday night swing as Evan pushed open the heavy oak door. A large oak bar divided the main room, formerly called the public bar, from the more genteel lounge, the former private bar, with its oak tables and fireplace. Both rooms were oak panelled and there was a fire going all year in the big fireplace. Loud conversation competed with Frank Sinatra on the jukebox. Llanfair wasn't very up-to-date in its musical taste. Cigarette smoke hung heavy in the air and a great burst of laughter erupted from the lounge next door as Evan came in. He looked around for Evans-the-Meat and the other usual customers, but he couldn't see them. A group of younger men, currently working on the road up from Llanberis, stood in the corner. Evan was wondering whether to join them when a clear high voice rang out.

"There he is, now. We were wondering where you had got to, Evan bach."

The voice belonged to the other complication in Evan's life. Betsy, the blond, voluptuous barmaid at the Red Dragon made it obvious that she fancied Evan and was determined to get him in the end. So far Evan had managed to worm his way out of her tempting invitations to foreign films and dances in Caernarfon, but Betsy still pursued him as eagerly as ever. Evan sometimes wondered whether his reluctance to tell her flat out that he wasn't interested was entirely due to not wanting to hurt her feelings. In fact he sometimes told himself he must be mad. Half the men in the village would have fought for a date with Betsy and even Evan had fantasised occasionally about what he might be missing.

It was warm in the bar and Betsy was wearing a black Lycra bodysuit with a black leather miniskirt. Around her waist was an absurdly small frilled white apron that would have protected nothing and made her look like a maid in a French farce. Evan was fairly sure that she wasn't wearing a bra under the bodysuit, and she also had the habit on leaning across the bar to chat with the customers, pulling her low neckline even lower.

She leaned forward now as Evan crossed the room, watching him with unabashed interest.

"I'm glad you've changed out of that stuffy old uniform," she said as he approached the bar. "That T-shirt looks good on you, Evan Evans. Shows off your muscles."

She glared fiercely at one of the young men who was nudging his mate and grinning. "Now what have I said that's so funny, Barry-the-Bucket?" she demanded. "I'm allowed to look at the merchandise if I'm shopping, aren't I?" She turned the full force of her gaze back to Evan. "All alone tonight then, are you, Evan bach? I suppose that Bronwen Price must be out birdwatching again? Lucky for me then. Pint of Guinness, is it?"

Evan was relieved that he hadn't been asked to contribute to the conversation until now.

"I thought I'd try the McAffreys tonight," Evan said, indicating the tap for the other Irish stout. "I feel like a change."

Betsy ran her tongue over her deep red lips. "I like a man who's always ready to experiment."

She put such overtones into this and gave Evan such a frank stare that he commented hastily, "I see the colonel's not in yet."

Betsy looked around. "That's right. I wonder where he's got to. It's not like him to miss opening time, either."

"I saw him up on the hill above Morgan's farm earlier,"

Evan said, "I hope nothing's happened to him. He's not as young as he thinks he is and that path is pretty steep in places."

"Oh, don't worry about him," Betsy said as she poured Evan's pint of beer. "He's as fit as a fiddle and you know it. And there's plenty of life in the old dog yet, if you get my meaning. I notice he always has a good look up my skirt when I have to get up on the stool to reach that shelf with the old single malt whiskeys on it—like some other people I might mention," she added, giving Evan another knowing stare, "and once when I was bending down, he pinched my bottom." She gave Evan a challenging smile.

Evan had just noticed that Betsy was wearing a long silver chain around her neck. Whatever was on the silver chain had disappeared into her cleavage. He tried to stop himself from speculating what the object might be.

"All the same," he went on, trying to steer the subject back into safer waters, "he's always here for opening time, isn't he?"

"How long ago when you saw him on the hill?"

"Must have been a good hour now."

"Well, there you are then," Betsy said. "It would have taken him a while to get down from Morgan's hill and you know how vain he is about his appearance. He'd have gone back to Owens' and changed his clothes, wouldn't he?"

Evan smiled. "You're probably right," he said.

"I'm usually right about most things," Betsy said, her eyes flirting with him. "Speaking of which, there's a new film I really want to see at the multiplex in Colwyn Bay. I thought that . . ."

Mercifully Evan was spared having to come up with an excuse by the arrival of a man carrying a tray of empty glasses. "Same again all around, Betsy love," he said, pushing the tray in front of her. "All Brains." He named the popular beer from Cardiff.

"All Brains and no brawn, is that what you're saying, Mr. Roberts?" Betsy quipped.

"Enough brawn among us to handle you, Betsy love," Roberts said, giving Evan a grin. "Evening, Constable Evans."

"Evening, Roberts-the-Pump," Evan said. Mr. Roberts owned Llanfair's only petrol station and garage. "What were you doing sitting in the lounge? Have you got visitors or have you gone all posh suddenly?"

"We're all in there with Ted Morgan," Roberts-the-Pump said. "We're doing a spot of reminiscing. We were all lads together at the school here once."

"Old Taff Morgan's son, you mean?" Evan was surprised.

"That's right."

"What's he doing here? I thought he never came near the place," Evan said. "I'd heard he hadn't been back for twenty years."

"That's right. Never came near the place." A man who had been standing silently beside the bar sauntered over to join them. He was wearing the typical farmer's outfit of tweed jacket, tweed cap, trousers tucked into socks so that he could ride his motorbike over his land, and very muddy boots. "Couldn't even show up for his own father's funeral, could he, and now he's inherited the farm, he turns up cool as a bloody cucumber, acting like the big shot from London, buying drinks all around."

There was real venom in his voice and Evan wondered for a second whether it was because he hadn't been included in the drinks all around. Then he remembered who he was—Sam Hoskins, a farmer down the valley near Beddgelert who was married to Taff Morgan's daughter.

Betsy leaned across the counter, stretching the bodysuit to dangerous limits. "No wonder you're upset, Sam. It doesn't seem fair, does it. They say he's already got property all over London and now he gets the farm too."

"He got everything, and my Gwyneth who looked after her old da and did his washing and darned his socks didn't even get a thank you note."

27

Evan looked at Sam in surprise. "I didn't know old Taff very well, but he seemed like a decent enough old bloke. Why would he leave it all to Ted?"

"That's easy," Betsy said. "He thought the sun shone out of Ted's head, didn't he? Every time he came in here he was always boasting about his son, the rich London businessman and all the property he owned and how he drove a Jaguar and flew to Paris for weekends. Ever so proud of Ted, he was. You should have seen him come in here all excited if Ted ever wrote to him."

"But why leave Ted the farm when it sounds like he was doing pretty well without it?" Evan commented. "He didn't think Ted would ever come back here and start farming, did he?"

Sam Hoskins snorted. "The silly old fool made a will years ago and never changed it. I suppose he was always hoping that Ted would get fed up with London and come home some day."

"Well, now he has," Robert-the-Pump said, "so I suppose it worked, didn't it?"

Betsy was filling one glass after another with expert ease, letting just the right amount of froth rise over the top. "He's never coming back here to live, is he?" she asked.

"He says he's going to give it a try," Roberts-the-Pump answered.

"A dump like this?" Betsy finished pouring the last glass. "What would he do with himself here? And what about his business in London?"

"If you really want to know," Roberts-the-Pump said, leaning confidentially close, "he's thinking of buying the old slate mine."

"But it's been closed since I was a little girl!" Betsy exclaimed, loudly enough to make everyone in the bar turn around and listen. "Ted Morgan is thinking of reopening the old slate mine?"

28

"What would he want to do that for?" someone muttered. "Wants his brains examined."

"I wouldn't say that. It would be good for Llanfair, wouldn't it?" Roberts-the-Pump said. "Think of all the extra trade."

"And all the jobs," Betsy said excitedly. "My old da hasn't worked since they closed the mine. He might want to go back."

"Your old da would rather sit home watching the telly and collect his dole, Betsy love," someone commented from the far corner by the fire. "You can't see him climbing up rock faces now, can you?"

"He'd still remember how," Betsy said haughtily. "He helps out with the mountain rescue, doesn't he, Evan?"

Evan nodded, reluctant to say that Betsy's father was usually well pickled with alcohol and more of a hindrance than a help to the mountain rescue squad.

"I'd imagine there are plenty of men around here who'd like their old jobs back," Betsy went on, leaning out across the bar and making every man in the place suddenly attentive. "It might bring some life to this dull old place too. Maybe they'd build a supermarket or one of those multiplex cinemas like in Colwyn Bay."

"You can imagine what Evans-the-Meat would have to say about that." Same Hopkins chuckled.

"He'd attack anyone with his meat cleaver who tried to put in a supermarket," commented Harry-the-Pub.

"I can't see how a smart London businessman would think that old mine was a good investment," the Rev. Parry Davies declared, coming out of the corner where he usually chose to sit hidden when drinking. "It was losing money long before they closed it."

"Maybe Ted Morgan feels guilty about having all that money and wants to do something nice for his community," Betsy suggested with her usual wide-eyed naïveté.

Sam Hoskins spluttered into his beer. "Him? When has he ever done something nice for anyone? He wouldn't even lend his own sister five hundred pounds when our sheep got that virus and we had those big vet bills."

The Rev. Parry Davies coughed. "I remember Ted Morgan when he was in my Sunday school class and I don't think that altruism was ever one of his stronger points."

"Come again?" Betsy looked blank. "Alt what?"

"Being nice to other people, Betsy," Rev. Parry Davies said. "I remember that Ted had the largest collection of marbles in the village, obtained by fair means and foul."

"Maybe he's seen the light, reverend," Roberts-the-Pump said as he picked up the tray of beers and headed back to the noisy party next door. "Maybe he's found religion, thanks to those-long-ago Sunday school classes." He turned to wink at Evan. "Why don't you come through and join us, Evans-the-Law? We've been telling Ted all about you."

"Only the good things, I hope," Evan said, glancing awkwardly at Sam Hoskins who stood, arms folded, glaring down at his big boots. "In a minute, maybe. I'm still wondering whether I should go check on the colonel. I've never known him as late as this."

As if on cue the door burst open and Colonel Arbuthnot rushed in, sweat pouring from his scarlet face.

"I've found it," he managed to gasp. "I've finally found it!"

Chapter 4

Evan let out a sigh of relief as the colonel staggered up to the bar. He couldn't think why he'd been so worried. The colonel spent every day tramping over the hills and nothing had ever happened to him yet. As Betsy said, he was as fit as a fiddle.

Harry-the-Pub hastily poured a generous tot of Scotch as the colonel leaned against the bar, his breath coming in deep gulps.

"Found what, colonel?" Betsy asked as Evan went to his aid.

The colonel tossed back the Scotch in one shot, shuddered, and took a deep, gasping breath. "King Arthur," he said. "I've finally found King Arthur's castle."

"I've noticed it myself a couple of times." One of the younger men chuckled. "A lot of turrets and flags flying, wasn't it?"

"Or maybe you're getting short-sighted, colonel, and you're mixing up King Arthur's castle with the Everest Inn," Barry, the local bulldozer operator, quipped, giving his companion a hearty dig in the ribs. "Easy enough to do, with all those flags and geraniums, eh?"

He looked pleased with himself as he grinned at the company.

"You keep quiet now, Barry-the-Bucket," Betsy said, frowning at the grinning man. "If the colonel says he's found King Arthur, he has."

"And was the round table in it?" Barry continued, undaunted.

"Tell us all about it, colonel," Betsy said encouragingly.

The colonel was still breathing hard and his face was still almost purple. "It's completely covered in gorse and bracken," he said. "So you could walk right past and not notice it. But it's very old, all right. Solid stone walls and a big stone on the floor. And just in the right position to guard the pass. It has to be a medieval fort."

"Where was this, colonel?" Evan asked, "Up above Morgan's farm where I saw you earlier?"

"Precisely," Colonel Arbuthnot said. "And not too far from the old slate mines. I must have walked past it a hundred times before and never noticed." He gasped for breath again. "I think I need another Scotch, Harry my good man. The excitement's all been too much." He took out an ancient silk handkerchief with moth holes in it and mopped his forehead. "I hurried all the way down and I would have come straight here, but I slipped on that confounded steep section and got mud on my trousers, so of course I had to pop into Owens' and change my clothes first."

Betsy gave Evan a knowing grin.

"This is most interesting," the Rev. Parry Davies said, coming to join them. "Most interesting indeed. We should notify the archaeology department at Bangor University in the morning."

"Why don't we go up and take a look at it now?" Barry-the-Bucket said.

"Tonight?" Betsy demanded.

"You want to make sure the colonel's really found some-

32

thing before you go calling up the professors at Bangor, don't you? And it won't be dark for another couple of hours," Barry said.

"But the colonel's tired. He won't want to go up there again."

"My dear Miss Betsy," Colonel Arbuthnot said, drawing himself up to his full stature, "never let it be said that a member of the Khyber Rifles was too tired for anything. Another Scotch and I could scale Mount Everest!"

He downed the shot in one gulp amid applause and was swept out of the pub on a noisy tide of Welshmen. Roberts-the-Pump put down his tray of beers. Some of the men from the next room came out to see what was happening.

"The colonel's found King Arthur's castle," Roberts-the-Pump yelled. "We're going up to take a look."

"King Arthur's castle? I don't believe it." Evans-the-Milk laughed.

"Well, I believe it," Evans-the-Meat said. "I always knew if they found King Arthur anywhere, they'd find him here, in Wales."

"Well, I'm not running up a mountain on a wild-goose chase," Evans-the-Milk said.

"Not up to it, are you?" Evans-the-Meat jeered. "But then I always said you came from the weaker side of the family, didn't I?"

"Who says I'm not up to it?" Evans-the-Milk demanded and joined the fight to get through the narrow bar door.

Like a pack of hounds on the scent they surged up through the village and on up the sheep path without slackening speed until after a stiff climb the colonel stood, breathing hard but triumphant at the site of his discovery. Willing hands wrenched away gorse and grasses.

"It's a ruin all right," Evans-the-Meat declared. "Good solid walls too. Just the kind of thing King Arthur would have built."

"But not very big, is it?" Barry-the-Bucket chuckled. "I mean, it would have to be a very small round table to fit in here, wouldn't it? There's less room to swing a cat in here than the bar down at the Dragon and that's saying a lot."

"It need not have been his main residence," Colonel Arbuthnot said. "This was obviously a guard post. But if we can find some artifacts . . ."

"Maybe a crown or two," Barry suggested, nudging his friends.

"Or a rotted wooden table?" One of the men chuckled.

"Or Excalibur would do nicely," another suggested.

"Just a minute. Quiet all of you," Rev. Parry Davies said with such authority that everyone fell silent. "I think we've made a significant find here. I have believed in the existence of this place and now I think we've found it at last."

"King Arthur's castle?" voices demanded in disbelief.

"No, not King Arthur's castle," Rev. Parry Davies said grandly. "This, my friends, is Gelert's grave."

There was stunned silence, then general laughter.

"What are you talking about, reverend?" someone demanded. "Everyone knows where Gelert's grave is. I've seen it myself, down beside the church in Beddgelert."

The reverend shook his head. "No, that was just a nineteenth-century confidence trick, a legend invented by a local innkeeper to attract tourists."

"You're saying Prince Llewellyn's dog Gelert wasn't really buried there?" Evans-the-Meat demanded.

"I'm saying that the dog Gelert probably didn't really exist," Rev. Parry Davies declared, "and almost certainly wasn't buried in a fancy grave."

"But the village has been called Beddgelert for hundreds of years," Evans-the-Milk said. "And even I, not speaking Welsh as fluently as Evans-the-Meat, know that the word means Gelert's grave."

"Precisely," Rev. Parry Davies said as if he had just scored a point. "It has long been assumed, in religious circles, that Gelert was the same as Saint Celert, an early Christian saint. He was reputed to have lived in a simple hermitage high on the pass so that he could be close to God. This little stone building would have been just about the right size for a hermitage, don't you agree?"

Several heads nodded.

"Too small for King Arthur, anyway," Barry-the-Bucket commented.

"And the big stone slab on the floor," Rev. Parry Davies went on, "surely that must be the saint's grave. The local people buried him here, where he was at home."

Evans-the-Meat pushed his way through the crowd until he was standing beside the minister. "So what you're saying is that Gelert wasn't really Prince Llewellyn's famous dog and Beddgelert doesn't really have Gelert's grave at all?" he asked.

"That is correct."

Evans-the-Meat let out a sudden whoop of laughter. "How about that, eh? This will be one in the eye for the folk down in Beddgelert, won't it? And it will put Llanfair on the map at last. Llanfair—home of Saint Celert's grave. We should call ourselves that, like that other Llanfair."

"You mean the other Llanfair over on Anglesey; the one that claims to have the longest name in the world?" Barry-the-Bucket asked.

"That's exactly what I mean," Evans-the-Meat said grandly. "If they can call themselves Llanfairpwllgwyngyllgogerychwyrndrobwllllantysiliogogogoch, which we all know means nothing more important than Saint Mary's church in the hollow of white hazel near the rapid whirlpool and Saint Tisilio's church near the red cave, then why shouldn't we start calling ourselves Llanfair-up-on-the-pass-with-the-brook-running-through-it-and-Saint-Celert's-grave-right-above-it?"

There was general laughter.

"You're not serious, man?" Barry-the-Bucket asked.

"Indeed I am," Evans-the-Meat replied. "It's about time we put our Llanfair on the map. Now that we've got the real Celert's grave, we've got something to shout about, haven't we?"

"You're sure it couldn't be a small fort?" Colonel Arbuthnot asked, the disappointment showing on his face.

Evans-the-Meat slapped him on the back. "A saint is just as good as a king, colonel bach," he said.

"Either way you've made an important discovery, colonel," Evan said. "We'll just have to wait and see what the trained archaeologists from Bangor say about it."

"I'm sure I'm right," Rev. Parry Davies said. "I've always thought that the saint's final resting place would be found one day."

"I thought Methodists weren't supposed to believe in saints?" Barry-the-Bucket chuckled.

"Of course we believe in holy men and women. We respect them for the lives they led. We just don't go praying to them like the heathen Catholics." He stood in the doorway to St. Celert's cell, head bowed with reverence. "And from what I've read, Saint Celert was among the most holy of the early Christians. I shouldn't be surprised if he didn't convert this whole valley himself, single-handedly."

"I've never heard of him," someone in the crowd muttered as they started down the mountain again.

"Then I think it behooves me to do a little research," Rev. Parry Davies said. "Yes, maybe I should write a simple life of Saint Celert. We could sell it, for a modest sum, when tourists want to visit."

"You should do an article in the North Wales weekly, reverend," someone suggested.

"That's right," Evans-the-Meat said proudly. "We should let the world know that Llanfair now has its own historic monument—just as long as the bloody tourists don't want to come and look at it."

The men walked down the mountain calling out absurd suggestions and laughing loudly.

"Don't forget to put in your book that the grave was discovered by the colonel, will you reverend?" Evan suggested, noting that the colonel had been walking along silent and tight-lipped.

"Of course he must," Barry-the-Bucket said, slapping the colonel on the back. "Go down in history, you will, colonel! They might want you to help them dig it up. I wonder if I could get my bulldozer up this path? That would speed things up, wouldn't it?"

"You don't excavate archaeological sites with a bulldozer, Barry-the-Bucket, man," Rev. Parry Davies exclaimed in horror.

Evan smiled as he fell into step beside the colonel.

"Maybe they could use an extra hand when they start excavating," Colonel Arthunot muttered to Evan, his good spirits revived. "I've always wanted to be in on a real dig. And if we actually find some artifacts . . ."

The sun had finally set behind the mountains, plunging the valley into deep gloom, as they dropped down the final steep section of path and came into the village. The higher slopes still glowed with evening light, tingeing the fleeces of the grazing sheep with pink. Evan looked around him with contentment.

"Going to be a beautiful day tomorrow," he said.

"It was lovely up here earlier," Colonel Arbuthnot commented. "So clear that you could see the ocean, and with my binoculars—good German ones, not this Japanese rubbish—I could see . . ." He paused, remembering just what he had seen. "You know, it was the most extraordinary thing," he went on, his loud voice booming as they walked down the street toward the Red Dragon, "but I thought I saw someone I recognized from somewhere else."

"Did you, colonel?" Evan asked politely.

The noisy crowd swept back into the pub, calling out their discovery to those who had stayed behind. Hands slapped the colonel on the back again and a double Scotch was shoved into his hand.

"This is the man who's going to put Llanfair on the map," Evans-the-Meat exclaimed proudly. "I've been thinking about it all the way down and I've decided we should call ourselves Llanfairbeddgelert, who-was-not-a-dog-but-a-saint-and-was-buried-high-on-the-pass-above-the-larch-trees-with-a-view-of-Snowdon. How does that sound then?"

"That's what we're going to call ourselves?" Harry-the-Pub chuckled. "My hand would get tired before I wrote all that."

"And the address wouldn't fit on a postcard," Betsy added.

"It would make us like that other Llanfair, the famous one," Roberts-the-Pump said. "What does that Llanfair have that we don't, except for the longest name in the world?"

"So we'll make ours one syllable longer," Evans-the-Milk suggested.

"Then we'd be famous!" Betsy exclaimed excitedly. "All the tourists would come here!"

"Hold on a second—who said anything about tourists?" Evans-the-Meat roared. "We just want the respect that is due to us, not hordes of bloody foreigners flocking here to take pictures."

"What's wrong with more tourists?" Evans-the-Milk demanded. "I for one would welcome more business."

"And I for one—" Evans-the-Meat began, raising his right fist in a threatening manner, until Evan stepped between him and Evans-the-Milk.

"Easy now, man," he said. "Everyone's entitled to an opinion. It's a free country, isn't it?"

"Not if I had my way," Evans-the-Meat remarked. "I'd get rid of all the bloody foreigners."

"Not the colonel, surely," said Barry-the-Bucket, "after he was the one who found your historic site for you?"

The reverend Parry Davies joined Evan between the two feuding men. "I suggest we have a village meeting to discuss calmly what this new discovery means to Llanfair and how we're going to proceed from here. Nothing should be said or done in haste. It's the grave of a saint we're talking about, not a tourist attraction. It should be treated with the utmost respect."

"You're right, reverend," Harry-the-Pub said. "So drink up, gentlemen, and let's leave the discussion until another time, right?"

Evan stepped aside and joined the colonel at the bar. He found his beer still standing there, only half-finished, its froth gone. He drained it. "We're a hot-headed lot, we Welsh, when our passions are roused." He grinned at the colonel. "The English have always found us hard to subdue."

"I felt the same about my wife," Colonel Arbuthnot said, smiling back. "She was Welsh, you know. Usually she was the most serene woman in the world, but when something upset her, watch out. I usually took a long walk until she had cooled off."

Evan chuckled. "So what did you start telling me about a strange person you had seen?" he asked.

"Oh, yes," Colonel Arbuthnot said. "It was most extraordinary. I was looking through the binoculars and I thought I recognized—" he broke off suddenly, staring out across the bar with a strange, almost embarrassed, look on his face. "I recognized a chap I used to know in India many years ago," he went on in a louder, heartier voice. "But of course it couldn't have been him. Poor old Monty Hallford broke his neck, falling off a polo pony back in thirty-nine!" He examined his watch. "Heavens, is that the time already? Mrs Owens will be wondering where I've got to and my dinner will be ruined. I really must go. See you chaps tomorrow then!"

39

He pushed his way through the crowd and hurried out of the bar, almost colliding with Annie Pigeon, who had just come in. Evan was glad to see that she had changed out of the skimpy shorts and was wearing an attractive sundress. The colonel hardly noticed her. He half muttered an apology and hurried on.

Evan stared after him with interest. What had made the colonel decide to leave in such a hurry?

Chapter 5

It was almost dark when Colonel Arbuthnot came out of the Red Dragon. As the cool night breeze blew in his face he slowed his pace. How stupidly he had behaved. He would never have held off that attack on the Afghan border if he'd lost his nerve so easily in those days. And anyway, what did he have to fear? They would pretend not to know each other and nothing would be said. He was perfectly safe, perfectly.

All the same, he glanced over his shoulder as he left the lights of the village behind and struck out on the path to Owens' farm. The path wound beside the stream, crossing it by a rather precarious little bridge. It wasn't easy to follow in the dark, but the colonel knew it well. He took the same route every night, rather than walk all the way through the village and then up the main track to Owens'. Usually he brought a flashlight with him, but he'd been in such a hurry tonight that he'd forgotten it.

He thought a twig snapped behind him and glanced over his shoulder again. Tree branches were moving in a ghostly dance. Pull yourself together, man, he told himself firmly. It was extraordinary what strange shapes trees could take on in the twilight. He broke into a trot again, taking out his silk handkerchief to mop at the sweat trickling down his forehead. Why should he feel threatened like this? Nothing to worry about. Over the bridge, across that last field, and he'd be home. He could see the welcoming light streaming from Mrs. Owens' parlor window. Tomorrow this would all seem rather amusing.

He sensed, rather than heard, someone moving behind him.

Evans-the-Post came out of the post office and general store with a bulging mailbag slung over his shoulder. A big smile spread across his vacant-looking face as he headed for the bridge. This was going to be a good day. There were several picture postcards among the mail he had to deliver and he could read those without anybody getting angry with him. And there was what looked like a wedding invitation for the Hopkinses. He'd have to find out who was getting married!

He glanced back to see if old Miss Roberts was watching him. She gave him a good scolding whenever she caught him reading the mail. "Crabby old woman," he muttered to himself. Getting a peek at other people's lives was one of the perks of being a postman, wasn't it? And he didn't mean any harm—everyone in Llanfair knew that.

The bridge was deserted and bathed in dappled sunlight as he loped toward it, his long limbs moving jerkily like an uncontrolled puppet. He was just about to settle himself when he glanced over the parapet to the rushing stream below. There was something moving in the water that glinted in the sunlight. It was cream-colored and shiny, moving gracefully among the reeds. At first Evans-the-Post thought that it was a new flower he'd never seen before. Some kind of water lily maybe. He decided to try and pick it. The policeman would know what it was, or the schoolteacher, if he wasn't too shy to ask her.

He left his mailbag beside the bridge and clambered down the steep bank. Holding onto one of the alder trees that grew there, he leaned out into the stream and reached for the flower. After a couple of attempts he grabbed it. His smile of triumph faded when he lifted it out and saw what it was. It wasn't a flower at all. It was a square of shiny, cream-colored fabric, silk maybe.

It was an odd thing to find in the river, knowing that there were just sheep pastures above it. Nobody could have dropped it from the bridge, that was clear, or it would have been swept downstream. Even Evans-the-Post could figure that out. He stared upstream to see where it might have come from. That was when he saw what at first he thought was an odd-shaped boulder with water splashing over it.

Evan opened his eyes to sunlight painting a bright stripe across the flowery wallpaper. Mrs. Williams must have forgotten to waken him. He was about to leap out of bed when he realized it was Saturday. He lay back with a sigh of contentment. Nothing on the agenda for the whole day. He would read the paper while eating a leisurely breakfast, and then he'd do some climbing. It was weeks since a free day and a fine day had coincided and he felt like a challenging climb, maybe on the cliffs below Glaslyn. He hadn't liked to go there since those two men fell to their deaths. But it was stupid to stay away from some of the best climbs in the area.

He got out of bed and a thought struck him—maybe Bronwen would be free today and might feel like going for a hike with him. They'd talked about hiking on the Llwyn Peninsula, where there was great birdwatching on deserted beaches.

He leaned on the window sill, an anticipatory smile on his face as he looked at the clear blue sky. Such days didn't happen often in North Wales, so you had to drop everything and make the most of them. He could smell bacon and sausage frying downstairs and the radio blaring out the usual Saturday morning music that Mrs. Williams liked—pop music from the fifties and sixties, Tommy Steele, Cliff Richard, and the Beatles.

The village street was slowly coming to life. Owens-the-Sheep went by on his motorbike, his black-and-white border collies running at his heels. Farmers never had a day off, did they? The milk van was halfway up the street and Evan heard the familiar chink of milk bottles. Evans-the-Milk didn't get many days off either. A couple of little boys ran up the hill dressed in their football uniforms. That reminded Evan that he did have a commitment—he'd more or less promised the boys that he'd go and watch their big game down in Beddgelert.

Never mind, the game would be over by noon and he'd still have half a day to do what he wanted . . . and Bronwen would definitely be at the game too. A good way to find out what her plans were.

He was about to turn away from the window when he saw an extraordinary sight. Evans-the-Post was running up from the bridge, his long limbs flying out, his head lolling from side to side as he ran, his mailbag dancing beside him, envelopes clutched in his hand.

Evan opened his window and leaned out. "Where's the fire, Evans-the-Post?" he called.

The mailman stopped, looking up at him with his mouth open. "It's no fire, man," he stammered. "There's something in the river, something you have to come and see right now!"

"Not again!" Detective Sergeant Watkins from the regional police headquarters in Caernarfon climbed out of the white police van.

Evan was waiting for him by the bridge with most of the village watching on from behind the yellow police tape he'd hastily put up. "Sorry to get you out on a Saturday, sarge," he said apologetically, "but I've got a suspicious death I thought someone ought to see."

"Do you always wait to find your bodies until I'm the only one on duty?" Sergeant Watkins growled. "I hoped I could go watch our Tiffany's football match this afternoon. She's turning into a good little player. Center forward. Pity she's a girl, in fact. I could have signed her up with Manchester United." He sighed. "Okay, so show me the body."

"We pulled him out of the river," Evan said hesitantly as he led the sergeant down the steep bank. "I hoped there might have been a chance we could revive him, but I'd wager he's been dead a while."

Ahead of them on the river bank a white sheet now covered the body of Colonel Arbuthnot. As they came closer, the wind lifted the corner of the sheet and the colonel's left hand, with gold signet ring, was suddenly visible. Sergeant Watkins pulled back the sheet and stared down at Colonel Arbuthnot's white, bloated face.

"Do you know who he was?" he asked sharply.

"Oh yes," Evan said. "His name was Colonel Arbuthnot."

"A local?"

"No, but well known around here. He's been spending a couple of weeks here every summer for the past ten years or so."

"Poor old chap," Sergeant Watkins said. This was one of the things Evan liked about Watkins—he still cared. Most policemen didn't, or pretended that they didn't. "Still I imagine he was getting on in years, wasn't he?"

"He had to have been at least eighty," Evan said. "He was out in India before World War Two."

"When was he last seen?"

"He left the pub about nine o'clock last night. I was there. I saw him leave. And apparently he always took a shortcut back to the Owens farm, where he stays. It goes behind the pub, along the riverbank and then crosses the river by that little bridge." Evan pointed upstream. The river had narrowed at that point and the bridge was scarcely more than planks laid between blocks of granite.

Sergeant Watkins stared at it for a moment, then looked back, tracing the colonel's route back to the Red Dragon.

"And he never made it home?"

"I can't tell you that," Even said. "Mrs. Owens, the farmer's wife he lodges with, said that she left a cold meal out for him in his own sitting room, so she had no idea whether he came in. They go to bed early on farms. The meal wasn't touched anyway."

"And the door was still unlocked?"

"They never lock doors. They've got dogs."

"So when did she find out he wasn't there?"

"She didn't. She said she was a little concerned that he was sleeping in so late, but she didn't like to check on him and risk waking him."

"So we can assume he didn't make it home last night," Sergeant Watkins said. "He'd been in the pub, you say? Drank a fair amount?"

"Four glasses of Scotch," Evan said. "But he usually got through at least that much in an evening. It never seemed to affect him. He could put it away with the best of them."

"All the same," Sergeant Watkins went on, "I can't quite see why you called us in on this. It's pretty obvious, isn't it? The old boy knocks back a few too many, his eyesight is probably poor and he loses his balance on the bridge. All it would take is a sudden gust of wind . . ."

"What about this, though?" Even turned the colonel's head gently and indicated an ugly wound behind his right ear.

"Simple enough," Watkins went on. "There are some pretty nasty-looking rocks down below that bridge. The old boy hit his head as he fell. He glanced up and saw Evan's face.

"What?" Sergeant Watkins grimaced. "Oh come on, you're not going to tell me that you suspect foul play, are you?"

"I wouldn't have called you if I didn't," Evan said.

"Do you find yourself another murder every couple of months so that you don't get bored up here?" Watkins was only half joking. "Now I'm the detective around here and I'd just love to know, what makes you think that this wasn't an accident?"

46

"This," Evan said. He indicated the front of the colonel's Harris tweed jacket. "See here. A couple of burrs and a foxtail caught in the tweed. He must have been lying in the grass before he was dragged into the water."

"Not necessarily," Sergeant Watkins said. "He could have taken off his jacket any time and laid it down on the grass. He could have sat on it, couldn't he? He might not have noticed a couple of tiny burrs for days."

Evan shook his head. "You didn't know the colonel. He always liked to look what he called well turned out. He went home to change his trousers because he got mud on them before coming to the pub last night. He'd never have left the house with bits of plant stuck in his jacket."

"We don't know how good his eyesight was."

"Damned good," Evan said. "He didn't miss a thing."

"So you're suggesting," Watkins said slowly, "that someone bashed this old man on the head and then shoved him into the river?"

"It seems that way."

"It seems bloody stupid to me," Sergeant Watkins said. "We're not in the backstreets of Cardiff here. People don't run around bashing old men over the head and tossing them into a river." He looked long and hard at Evan. "You were right about the murders last time, but I can't go along with this. Not unless you can tell me that you've got a raving lunatic running around the neighborhood or that someone had a score to settle with the old boy."

Evan shook his head. "That's the problem, sarge. As I said, he was well liked here. He was treated like a kind of village mascot."

"So if anyone did kill him, they were taking a hell of a risk," Watkins said. "Any passerby would have noticed if the old chap was being followed, wouldn't they?"

Evan sighed. "Like you said, this isn't Cardiff, sarge," Evan said. "Most people are inside with their doors shut and curtains drawn by nine o'clock, and the others were in the pub." He paused to think. "In fact almost all the men of the village were in the pub last night when the colonel went home."

"You think it would have to have been a man?"

"It would take a pretty strong woman to make that dent in his skull and then drag his body into the river."

Sergeant Watkins laughed uneasily. "Come on, Evans. You know what Detective Inspector Hughes is like. He's at a conference in Colywn Bay all day but he gave me strict instructions to page him if anything came up. I don't really have the authority to do anything without him, do I? And he gave me a hell of a time when he thought I'd let you stick your nose in those other murders."

"So you want me to turn the other way and call this an accident just so that we don't upset D.I. Hughes?" Evan asked.

"I'm going to call it an accident," Sergeant Watkins said. "Unless you can give me any evidence to the contrary, apart from some bits of plant sticking to his jacket—which might have got there when you dragged him out of the river."

Evan shook his head. "We lifted him out and laid him here."

"Can you give me a single reason that anyone would want to kill him?"

"No," Evan said after a pause. He was thinking of the colonel's exit from the pub last night, the strange look that had come over his face and the way he had started babbling about that ridiculous story. Something had rattled the old man, that was clear. He had left in a hurry because he was upset—so upset that he had nearly knocked over Annie Pigeon as she was coming in, and he had scarcely waited to apologize. Given his old-world chivalry, that seemed significant. But it still was far from proof that his life was in danger.

"No, nothing at all," Evan repeated. This was something he'd have to look into for himself.

"There you are then." Sergeant Watkins let out a sigh of relief.

"But we can't just write this off, sarge," Evan insisted. "What if there's a murderer here?" He paused then added, as Sergeant Watkins was pulling the sheet over the body again, "You didn't want to think those two deaths on Mount Snowdon were murders either, did you?"

"All right. Don't rub it in," Watkins growled good-naturedly. "I know: You were right and I was wrong. Okay, this is what we'll do. I'm willing to call this death suspicious, because of the trauma to the head. That means the body will be sent off to the Home Office pathologist in Bangor. Let's see what he thinks caused the blow to the head. If he thinks there's anything fishy about it, we'll take it further."

"When will we know?" Evan walked beside the sergeant back to his white police van.

"He won't get to it until Monday."

"Monday?"

"Hold your horses. I can't call him in at the weekend, away from his fishing, can I? Not unless I was a hundred percent sure we'd got a crime. Everything will keep until Monday."

"But what about the crime scene," Evan said, looking back at the yellow tape. "There might be valuable clues that could be tampered with."

"We'll keep the tape up," Watkins said. "Tell the locals we have to determine how he fell into the river before we can open up the path again."

"Thanks, sarge."

"And in the meantime, Evans," Sergeant Watkins muttered as they approached the crowd behind the yellow tape, "I wouldn't give any hints that you suspect foul play. This was a tragic accident, nothing more. Got it? We don't want people panicking unnecessarily, do we?"

"No, sarge," Evan said. He was thinking that it would give

him some time to do some unofficial snooping. It would also put a killer at his ease. And when people relaxed, they sometimes slipped up.

"Oh, and, Evans," Sergeant Watkins added as he climbed into the van, "no playing at detective on you own, understand me? You don't touch anything until you get the go ahead from me, got it?"

"Very good, sir," Evan said, giving a friendly wave as the van revved and eased its way through a crowd of curious onlookers.

But that doesn't stop me from using my eyes and asking a few questions, Evan thought to himself.

Chapter 6

But by the end of Saturday Evan still had no other shred of evidence to convince Sergeant Watkins that they were dealing with more than an accident—apart from his own gut feeling. And he didn't feel that they were dealing with the random act of a lunatic either. It was more sinister and more deliberate than that. For some reason someone had wanted the colonel silenced. Evan couldn't think why. It was strange that his death had come immediately after his momentous discovery on the mountain, but Evan couldn't imagine why the discovery of an old ruin would drive anyone to kill. If he'd been killed to prevent him from making a discovery—that would make sense. But this murder made no sense at all.

He had racked his brains all afternoon but couldn't come up with anyone in Llanfair who didn't like the colonel. The old man had been a popular figure in the village. To Evan's knowledge he had never fallen out with anyone.

This was borne out by the genuine sadness Evan noticed as the colonel's body was collected to be taken to the pathologist in Bangor. The local people stood watching silently. Men in the crowd removed their caps. Women dabbed at their eyes. Evan glanced around, trying to observe the crowd and note who was present, who was missing.

"Are you going to take the tape down now?" one of the little boys asked Evan as the van drove away.

"Not yet. We have to leave it up for the time being." Evan raised his voice a little. "We need to find out just how and where he fell into the river, so that we can prevent any more accidents like this, don't we?"

He started to move among the crowd, asking questions. On the pretext of asking people if they remembered what time the colonel left the pub, Evan managed to compile a pretty accurate list of who was there that night. The list included almost all the men of the village, plus some of the women as well. The only men not present were a couple of young lads out on dates, some fathers home with their wives, and the Rev. Powell-Jones who, unlike his rival at the other chapel, never touched the demon alcohol.

That meant that almost every able-bodied man in the village had a cast-iron alibi for that night. Most of them had seen the colonel leave the pub, but nobody saw what happened after that. As Evan had guessed, all the other inhabitants of Llanfair were safely indoors with curtains drawn at nine o'clock.

It was late Saturday afternoon when Evan finished interviewing the villagers and went to talk to Mrs. Owens, the colonel's landlady. He skirted the police tape along the riverbank but crossed the river by the same little bridge from which the colonel had plunged to his death. Evan stood on the planks that spanned the stream, watching the water cascade over the rocks. It was true that the colonel could have hit his head if he had fallen onto those rocks, and the rushing water would have wiped away any trace of blood. But the bridge really wasn't unstable, and it was wide enough for a man to cross safely, unless he was very drunk indeed.

Mrs. Owens was quite distraught when she opened the front door. She dabbed her eyes with a sodden handkerchief as she led him into her kitchen and offered him a seat at the scrubbed pine table. Evan looked around with approval, thinking that this was just how a farm kitchen should look. One wall was taken up with an enormous Welsh dresser containing a set of willow pattern plates, another wall was dominated by a big cast-iron stove, now superseded by the smart electric range beside it. The walls were whitewashed stone and the floor well-scrubbed gray slate. The whole place was spotless. No wonder the colonel felt so comfortable here.

"We ought never to have shown him that shortcut." Mrs. Owens sniffed as she poured Evan a cup of tea without asking. "It's our fault. We should have known an old man like that could have lost his balance on that bridge. I kept telling Mr. Owens that it was rickety and needed repairing, but you know how busy he is." She blew her nose noisily.

Evan nodded with sympathy. "Don't upset yourself," he said. "I've been across the bridge. It's just fine and the colonel was as surefooted as an old goat, wasn't he? Look where he hiked in the mountains and never had any mishaps."

He stopped talking, staring out of Mrs. Owens' window at the green slopes that rose steeply. Surely if anyone had wanted to kill the colonel, it would have been much less risky to have done it up there. It would have been the simplest thing in the world to have followed him up into the high country and waited for the right moment to push him over a cliff. No one would ever have disputed that was an accident. So why risk doing it so close to the village?

". . . and he was always so happy here." Evan came back from his thoughts to hear Mrs. Owens in the middle of a sentence.

"I'm sorry, I was thinking about something," he said. "What were you saying?"

"Just that he always came here looking so peaky and down at the mouth and he perked up right away," Mrs. Owens said. "I don't think he had much to live for in London."

"Did he talk to you much about his life in London?" Evan asked.

"I didn't like to ask," Mrs. Owens said. "He was a paying guest, after all. It wouldn't have been proper to gossip. But I know it wasn't much. He had his walks around the park and the library and his club, maybe a night out at the pictures once a week. Not much of a life, poor man. He'd outlived all his friends and relatives, look you."

"So he didn't get any visitors then?"

"Never had a visitor in all the years he's been here."

"And what about letters? Did he get letters or phone calls from London?"

"Nothing. The poor man had nobody in the world, did he?"

"It seemed that way," Evan said. He got up from the hard kitchen chair. "At least you made his last days happy, Mrs. Owens. That's something worth thinking about, isn't it?"

Mrs. Owens nodded and blew her nose again before she got up and opened the door for him. He retraced his steps across the Owenses field, pausing to stare up at the slopes above where the colonel had made his great discovery. Was there any way that his death could have had something to do with that? Had somebody not wanted him to find the ruin? If so, then they were too late, weren't they? Now the whole village knew about it, and they were excited about it too.

Evan lay awake thinking most of the night. The colonel had had no enemies, no friends either. His only encounters seemed to be in the pub, but there was nobody he knew well. Not well enough to make him a target for murder. Nothing made sense.

Who would possibly benefit from his death? That was the first question they always taught you to ask in detective training. The colonel had outlived his family and friends. He had no fortune to leave to anyone. In fact Evan got the feeling that the colonel had just about made do on his pension. His well-worn clothing attested to that. Not exactly the kind of man who got bumped off for his money—unless he was one of those old eccentrics who lived like paupers but had pound notes stuffed in the mattress. Even knew that such people existed, but he doubted that the colonel had been one of them. For one thing the colonel was a generous man. He had never been slow to return hospitality in the pub. Oh well, no use speculating until they had the pathologist's report on Monday. He could be quite wrong . . .

Sunday dawned clear and bright and Evan looked out of his window wondering if he should even think about taking a day off. Would it be too crass and unfeeling to go out hiking the day after the colonel's death? Might someone dare to cross the police tape and tamper with the site while he was gone? Was it possible that he'd be needed if some kind of evidence turned up?

Then he reminded himself that he wasn't a detective, in fact he had been told to mind his own business and not do any detecting on his own. If they were dealing with a murder, he had done what was required of him—he had alerted the criminal investigation unit in Caernarfon and now it was up to them. He was a humble bobby and it was his day off.

He put on his climbing boots and went downstairs. There was no radio playing in the kitchen. Mrs. Williams greeted him with a somber nod. She was dressed in black and she looked in horror at his sweater and cords.

"You're never going up to the mountains today, Mr. Evans?" she asked in a shocked whisper. "And the poor colonel not even buried decently yet?"

Evan shrugged. "There's nothing I can do, is there, Mrs.

Williams? And I'm sure the colonel wouldn't mind if I went out walking. After all, it was what he loved doing best."

"That's true enough," Mrs. Williams nodded. "A kind of tribute to him, then, poor dear man." She took out a handkerchief and dabbed at her eyes. "Such a terrible tragedy. I always said that little bridge was unsafe. Why couldn't he have gone up the road instead of taking that stupid shortcut. Then he'd be with us still." She fought to control herself. "Life must go on," she said stiffly. "You'll be wanting your breakfast then, is it?"

"Just some toast will do," Evan said. He was really looking forward to bacon, sausage, and the works, but for once it didn't appear that these were being offered.

Mrs. Williams nodded as if toast was a fitting meal for those in grief. "I'll make you some toast, then I must be away off to chapel," she said, cutting off two large slices of bread. "You're not coming to chapel then?"

"Not this morning," Evan said. "I'll probably go tonight."

"I hope you men will have the decency not to go sneaking round to the pub after chapel," Mrs. Williams said.

"Us? Sneak to the pub? Whatever gave you that idea?" Evan asked innocently.

Mrs. Williams sniffed. "You think we don't see you? There's not much goes on in this village that isn't common knowledge, Mr. Evans. And I think you should respect the colonel's memory for once and not go drinking on the Sabbath."

Evan thought of saying that he thought it was likely the colonel would have approved of everyone having a drink in his memory, but he swallowed back the words at the last minute. They took death very seriously in Llanfair.

"So do you think they'll postpone the village meeting tomorrow night?" he asked.

Mrs. Williams shook her head. "Not from what Reverend Parry Davies was saying. He said he thought we should forge ahead as the colonel would have wished—although I don't exactly see what we need a meeting about. I mean, either the ruin turns out to be the saint's grave or not."

"There's more to it than that, Mrs. Williams," Evan said. "There are all sorts of crazy ideas floating around about changing Llanfair's name."

"Changing our name? What on earth to?"

Evan grinned. "Who knows? They started by suggesting that we now call ourselves Llanfair BG, short for Llanfair Bedd Gelert."

"Like they do with Llanfair PG, instead of having to say the whole long mouthful?"

"Exactly. And then someone wanted to make it longer than that other Llanfair, so that we can get into the Guinness book of records."

"I've heard some daft things in my time, but that takes the cake." Mrs. Williams sniffed. "Getting too big for their boots, that's what they are, and no good ever comes of that. I think I'll go to that meeting and tell them so."

"You do that, Mrs. Williams," Evan encouraged, smiling.

Mrs. Williams didn't smile. "Sometimes it needs a woman to make men see sense," she said. "You wait till you're married, young man. Then you'll find out—which reminds me. Now what does it remind me of?"

Evan could guess what was coming next. If he wasn't careful he was going to be set up for another encounter with Sharon.

"My toast isn't about to burn, is it?" he asked quickly. "Don't worry. I can get it. You best hurry to chapel or you'll be late."

"Well, if you're sure you'll be alright," Mrs. Williams said hesitantly. "I don't like leaving you to fend for yourself."

"I'll be fine. Off you go," Evan encouraged.

He sighed with relief as the front door closed and settled down to toast and Mrs. Williams' homemade marmalade.

He found he didn't have much of an appetite after all, so

he cleaned up the breakfast table and was well away from the house before Mrs. Williams returned from chapel. Not that she'd be back in a hurry today, he decided. With the tragedy to the colonel and the upcoming village meeting, there would be more to gossip about than usual this morning.

Evan paused as he crossed the bridge. The water splashed and sparkled among the rocks as if there had never been a tragedy further upstream. He gazed at the police tape still sealing off the bank where the colonel's body had lain. He was tempted to examine the area for blood spots or signs of a heavy body being dragged, just in case the rain came in before the lab boys got there. One good Welsh rain would wash any evidence away. But then he reminded himself that D.I. Hughes had a very short temper and had told Evans once before that he'd be in serious trouble if he interfered again.

Evan sighed and walked on. It was times like this that made him regret dropping out of detective training.

"Yoo-hoo! Evan!" He looked up as he heard his name being called and saw that Annie Pigeon was hurrying down the street toward him, dragging a reluctant Jenny beside her.

"Lovely morning, isn't it?" she asked as she stopped beside him. "Are you going walking?"

"I was thinking about it."

"I thought we might go for a little walk ourselves," Annie said cautiously. "Although I'm a bit nervous about going up to the hills by myself."

"Oh, it's quite safe," Evan said. "I wouldn't worry."

"That wasn't what I meant." Annie's voice had just a tinge of sharpness. "I meant about getting lost and falling down old mines. I've never lived in a place like this before. I don't know a thing—which paths are safe, which plants are safe, whether sheep attack you . . ."

She gazed up hopefully at Evan. "What I really need is a

guide who knows the place. You wouldn't like to have us tag along would you—just this first time, so that we get the hang of it?"

He wouldn't get much of a hike with the pair of them tagging along, Evan thought. Then he decided he was being selfish. Of course she needed someone to show her which paths were easy and which were dangerous.

"I'd be glad to," he said gallantly. "Are you ready to go now?"

"Why not? Don't you think we're dressed right?"

She was wearing a shiny red track suit which somehow didn't clash with her red hair. Jenny was all girl today, dressed in a pretty cotton dress with big puffed sleeves and a pink ribbon in her hair. Evan looked at their clean white shoes.

"Normally I wouldn't go up there without a rainproof jacket, but it's not going to rain for a while and I don't imagine we'll be going too far with the littl'un along."

"Oh, she might look frail, but she's tough like her mum, aren't you, Jenny?" When Jenny said nothing, she jerked her arm. "Go on, say hello to the nice policeman."

Jenny looked down and studied her white shoes.

"You daft thing," Annie said. "You were so excited when I said we were going to see him, weren't you? She does nothing but talk about you at home. She tells me over and over how you saved her. She thinks you're a proper hero. I think so too. And I don't think I ever thanked you properly, did I?"

"I was only doing my job." Evan gave her an embarrassed grin.

"You saved my kid's life and that's all that matters to me," Annie said. "She means the world to me, you know. She's everything."

Evan held out a hand to help her over the stile that straddled a dry stone wall. She took his hand daintily and Evan noticed her beautifully manicured red nails. Definitely a city girl.

59

Again he was curious about what had made her think of a spot like Llanfair. She was just stepping down the other side of the stile, still clutching onto Evan's hand, when someone came down the street toward them, walking quickly. Evan looked up and saw that it was Bronwen.

Chapter 7

"I went to your house but there was no one there," Bronwen said as she approached. She sounded calm enough but her cheeks were pink. "I thought we might take that hike over to Llyn Ogwen that we've been talking about, but I see you're busy."

She wasn't wearing her usual long flowing skirts and ethnic blouses but instead well-cut twills and a cornflower-blue shirt that exactly matched her eyes. Evan swallowed hard. "I—that is Annie asked me to show her around a little." He paused, looking from Annie, whose hand was still gripping his, to Bronwen, who was standing there with her hands on her hips.

"I don't think you've had a chance to meet Annie Pigeon yet, have you, Bron?" he asked. "She's just moved here."

"Is that right?" Evan knew that she was deliberately not making it easy for him.

"Annie, this is Bronwen Price, our schoolteacher. Jenny will be going to her school if you stay here long enough."

"Miss Price, eh? I've heard about you," Annie said. She released her grip on Evan and extended a hand to Bronwen. "Pleased to meet you, love."

Bronwen shook her hand.

"Annie's never had a chance to go mountain walking before," Evan said, "So I thought I ought to show her the easiest paths. You want to come with us?"

"I don't think so, thanks," Bronwen said. "I think I'll tackle the Llyn Ogwen hike on my own then. I've been wanting to do it for a while. Have fun." She hoisted her pack higher on her shoulders and strode off.

"Oh dear," Annie said. "I've messed things up for you there, haven't I? If looks could kill, I'd be in a pine box by now." She gave Evan a little shove. "Go on, go with her if you like. Jenny and me can find our own way around. We're not stupid."

"It's okay," Evan said, trying to sound more confident than he felt. "Bronwen and I will have plenty of weekends to go hiking together. She can spare me for one Sunday, I'm sure."

"I wouldn't want to spoil things for you," Annie said. "I'll go see her if you like and tell her that I was only asking for your help because you're the one person who has been friendly to me so far."

"There's nothing to spoil," Evan said. "Bronwen and I are just friends."

"Just good friends, huh?" Annie chuckled. "That's what they always say in the tabloids isn't it—usually just after the cameraman has caught them in bed together!"

"As I said," Evan continued, embarrassed by the way the conversation was going, "we enjoy each others company and we like the same things, but it hasn't gone any further than that."

"Then you'd better get moving, hadn't you?" Annie said, raising a challenging eyebrow. "Or maybe there's someone else you've got your eye on. The barmaid, for example? She's got all the right things in the right places, hasn't she—and doesn't mind showing them."

Evan laughed uneasily. "Betsy's a nice girl," he said, "but not my type."

62

"What *is* your type then?"

"I haven't quite decided," Evan said cautiously. He wasn't going to bare his soul to this woman he had just met. But as they continued up the track he asked himself the same question, and most of the answers seemed to point to Bronwen. He'd have to explain to Bronwen and make her understand that Annie Pigeon was no threat. He had no interest in Annie other than a professional one. The sooner he got her settled into village life, the better for all of them.

"I saw you braved the pub on Friday night," he said. "I was going to buy you a drink, but when I looked for you, I couldn't find you."

"I changed my mind," she said. "I thought it might be a good idea to go down to the pub and meet people, but when I got there, I saw it was all men, so I beat a hasty retreat. I didn't want to start off here with the wrong sort of reputation, did I?"

"The women usually go and sit in the lounge," Evan said, "but you're right. It's mostly men in the pub. We're still rather old fashioned here in Llanfair, and rather hypocritical too. The pubs have been allowed to open on Sundays for a few years now, but Sunday drinking is still officially frowned upon."

"So nobody drinks on Sundays?"

"I didn't say that." Evan grinned. "Everyone sneaks out of the back door of chapel and takes the footpath to the back door of the pub."

Annie laughed, then a horrified look crossed her face. "Oh Lord, I'm not expected to go to chapel, am I?"

"You've got a good excuse. You don't speak Welsh. The reverend Parry Davies gives his sermons in English sometimes, but not always. And attendance is dropping off too. None of the young people go now. Pity really."

"What—that they don't want to listen to boring old sermons?"

"No, that traditions die out."

63

Annie stopped and breathed hard. "Phew. It's quite a climb, isn't it?"

Evan didn't like to tell her that they hadn't really begun climbing yet. This was just the first sheep pasture. The real mountains rose sheer behind them. It took a long while before they finally reached the top of the pasture.

"There you are," he said as the village spread out below them. "Now you get your first good view."

"It's lovely," she said, smiling. "Doesn't the village look small? Like dollhouses, isn't it, Jenny love? Imagine that we've come all the way up here!"

"I'm tired, Mummy," Jenny complained.

Annie looked apologetically at Evan. "She's only got little legs and she's not used to walking. Neither am I, for that matter."

"Maybe we should cut back from here through Morgan's farm," Evan said. "The path gets pretty steep after this. See how it goes up past those rocks?"

"You mean people actually walk up there?"

"Oh yes," Evan said. "This path goes over that ridge and joins up with one of the main routes up Snowdon."

"I think I'll leave that for a while," Annie said, still breathing heavily. "I need to get in shape first. And we need to get you some proper walking shoes, Jenny. You've got mud all over those nice white ones."

Evan was curious to know how she managed financially. The little girl was beautifully dressed. Maybe there was a Mr. Pigeon paying child support after all. But he didn't ask. He didn't want to do anything that encouraged intimacy with Annie right now.

He led her down a gentle grade that dropped steadily to the village again. Ahead of them was a solid-looking, gray stone farmhouse, and beyond it a row of new glass and wood bungalows.

"This is Morgan's farm," Evan said. "Those are the holiday homes Ted Morgan had built this spring."

"Is that where the poor old bloke was staying?" Annie asked. "The one who fell in the river?"

"No, that was Owens' on the other side of the valley," Evan said. "See over there, just up from the river."

"And he fell off that little bridge?" Annie asked, squinting into the sunlight to focus on it. "It's not surprising, is it? I don't think I'd want to go home that way in the dark."

"The colonel usually carried a torch in his pocket," Evan said. "He was so excited that night that he forgot it."

"About finding that ruin?" Annie asked. "Doesn't sound too exciting to me to find a few old rocks."

Evan was focussing on the riverbank too. It was a good place to lie in wait for someone, hidden among all those trees and shrubs. The only buildings close to it were the pub, the police station, and the petrol pump. No houses nearby. The noise of water would have drowned any cry. A perfect spot to kill.

A loud scream made him start. Jenny rushed to her mother and clutched at her legs, clawing to be picked up.

"She's scared of the sheep now," Annie explained as a large sheep ambled past them.

"Sheep won't hurt you, Jenny," Evan said. "That sheep only came after you the other time because she thought you were taking her baby away. Your mummy would chase off anybody who tried to pick you up, wouldn't she?"

"See, love? Listen to what the nice policeman says," Annie soothed. "He'll take care of you. He won't let anything bad happen."

As they approached the farmhouse, they heard the sounds of hammering inside, and a tall, huskily built man came out carrying a sheet of plywood. He stopped and looked up when he saw them approaching.

"Hello there," he said. "Constable Evans, isn't it? We never did get to meet properly the other night at the pub." He came over, hand extended. "I'm Ted Morgan, old Taff's son."

"Pleased to meet you, Ted," Evan said. The man had a firm handshake. Although at first glance he looked like any other villager with sleeves rolled up and a cap on his head, Evan noted that the shirt he was wearing was Ralph Lauren and the shoes were Timberlands. "And this is Annie Pigeon. She's just moved here. Annie, this is Ted Morgan. He's a business tycoon from London."

He thought he saw a flicker of interest? amusement? in Ted's eyes. Then he said formally, "How do you do, Miss Pigeon. Or is it Mrs.?"

"It's Ms.," Annie said firmly.

"So you've come to live in Llanfair too? What a coincidence."

"Don't tell me you're coming to live here too, Mr, er, Morgan, is it?" Annie asked.

"I thought I'd give it a try for a while. The old man never did much with all this property. It would be a challenge to see what I could do with it. And I've had enough of London. I have a hankering for the simple life."

"The simple life." Annie said. "Isn't that what we all want?"

"And you've moved here from where?"

"Manchester," Annie said. "I come from Manchester."

"You've lost your accent."

"So have you, Mr. Morgan," Annie retorted. "No one would think you were Welsh."

Evan looked from one to the other. He could sense something going on here, but he wasn't sure what. Attraction? All he knew was that Annie hadn't been as polite or formal with him.

Jenny grew tired of standing still and wandered on ahead down the path.

"Jenny, wait for us, love," Annie called out. "Don't go wandering off."

Ted Morgan's eyes followed the child with interest. "Your little girl?" he asked.

"That's right." Her eyes looked at him defiantly.

"Pretty little thing," he said. "You're smart to keep a close eye on her. You never know when accidents can happen to little kids, do you? Even in a place like Llanfair."

"That's what I was telling her the other day, wasn't it, Annie?" Evan asked.

"What?" Annie asked, suddenly realizing he had spoken to her. "Sorry, I was watching Jenny. I'd better go after her. Excuse me."

She pushed past the two men and almost ran after Jenny.

Ted Morgan grinned at Evan. "Good-looking girl, isn't she?" he asked. "I wonder what made her come here? Maybe to find herself a steady bloke like you."

"I got the feeling she was eyeing you," Evan retorted.

Ted shook his head. "Funny—I didn't get that feeling at all. Anyway, one lot of alimony is enough for me. With any luck my ex wife won't be able to find me here."

He laughed. "Oh well, better get back to work, I suppose."

"Are you remodeling?"

"Remodeling? The place was uninhabitable. I've had to gut it and start from square one. They didn't build these old farmhouses for comfort, did they? And you should see the bathroom! I might want rural peace and quiet, but I like my comforts too. I'm living in one of my holiday cottages until it's finished."

"And you're doing it yourself?"

Ted Morgan grimaced. "I thought I might get started on it myself. I've got the contractors who built my bungalows coming in on Monday. But I've just found out I'm bloody useless at it. I've already hit my thumb with the hammer twice. Have you ever hit yourself with a hammer? Blood every-

67

where—you'd have thought it was a major crime scene." He started to walk away and gave Evan an easy wave. "See you in the pub tonight, maybe."

"Probably not tonight," Evan said. "After my landlady's stern warning about paying respect to the dead, I think I'd better stay away from the Dragon tonight. But some other time maybe."

"Respect for the dead?" Ted asked. "Oh, you mean the old bloke who fell into the stream?"

Evan nodded.

"But he was only a visitor, wasn't he?"

"It doesn't matter. Everyone liked him. The whole village is upset about it."

Ted Morgan shook his head in disbelief. "He had to go some time, didn't he—and falling off a bridge and hitting his head on a rock was as good as any. At least it was quick. The poor old bloke didn't have to lie there suffering in a hospital like a lot of them do."

"That's true," Evan said, "But he still loved life, you know."

Ted shifted uneasily. "Yeah, well, I'll buy you a beer another time then. I always make sure I start off by bribing the local police." He grinned, nodded, and went back inside.

Evan watched him go back into the farmhouse. A pleasant enough chap, he thought, but clearly not on the same wavelength as the villagers. He found himself echoing the question Ted had asked about Annie—I wonder what made him come back here?

There was no sign of Annie by the time he had finished talking to Ted Morgan. She must have decided to take Jenny home. Evan wondered if he had a chance of catching up with Bronwen on her hike. He was unlikely to catch her before she reached Llyn Ogwen but she'd probably stop there for lunch.

So he hurried in that direction and reached Llyn Ogwen, only to find no sign of Bronwen there. He had no way of knowing which route she'd take back to the village, and suddenly he felt angry with himself for following her in the first place. It was like admitting he was wrong and feeling guilty, wasn't it? He hastily retraced his steps back to the village by the route he had come.

That evening he intercepted her as she came down from the mountains, making sure he was out in the village street as she came past.

"Had a good hike?" he asked casually.

Her face was glowing with sun and excitement. "Wonderful," she said. "Pity you couldn't have been there. I saw two mountain goats and a fox. But then I expect you saw quite a bit of wildlife of your own."

She went to walk past him. Even grabbed her arm. "Bronwen, you've nothing to be jealous about, you know."

Her face really flushed then. "You're right," she said. "I've nothing to be jealous about, have I? I'm only a friend, like any other person in this village. In fact you're probably only being nice to me because it's your job."

"You know that's not true, Bron."

"So tell me why I should think I'm in any way special to you?" she demanded. "We've never even been on a date together."

"We've been out walking enough."

"You go out hiking with anyone who has the time to go with you. You've been up to the mountains with old Charlie Hopkins."

Evan took a deep breath. "So where would you want to go?"

"Somewhere fancy. Somewhere special." Bronwen brushed stray wisps of corn-colored hair from her face.

"I didn't think you were the kind of person who liked fancy places."

"I'd like to be asked," she said, and the ghost of a smile crossed her face.

"There's a new Italian restaurant opened in Conwy," Evan said cautiously. "I hear it's pretty good. Would you like to go there to dinner some time?"

"That would be very nice," she answered. "Just as long as you're not thinking of inviting Annie to make up a threesome."

"I was thinking of asking Betsy as well. I hate uneven numbers."

Bronwen had to smile.

"Next Saturday maybe?" Even suggested.

"Alright."

Evan watched her walk away. He loved the easy grace with which she moved, the way her long braid swung behind her with a life of its own. It was only when he was back inside the house that the full impact of their conversation hit him. Now you've done it, he told himself. Dinner at an Italian restaurant definitely qualified as a date. And no matter how careful they might be, the village would hear about it and he'd be as good as engaged in their eyes. Still, it had to happen sometime, didn't it? He couldn't keep away from women forever.

Chapter 8

"Mr. Evans—look you here! You'll never believe it!" Mrs. Williams' shrill voice echoed up the narrow stairs as Evan was shaving on Monday morning. Hastily he dried his face and hurried downstairs, not knowing what he was going to find. With Mrs. Williams the summons could mean anything from a new rose on her bush to Martians landing in the street outside.

"What's happening then?" Even burst into the kitchen.

"Look you here!" Mrs. Williams repeated, waving the newspaper at him. "It's all here in black and white. We're famous."

Evan took the paper from her. On the front page, right under the banner "*The Daily Post*. Newspaper for North Wales," was a headline that said, "MAJOR ARCHAEOLOGICAL DISCOVERY WILL PUT LLANFAIR ON THE MAP."

"Put us on the map, that's what it says." Mrs. Williams put her hands to her ample bosom in excitement. " 'Deed to goodness. Who would have thought it?"

Evan scanned the column quickly. "It says the find still has to be verified by archaeologists from the university," he said.

"Yes, but look you what else it says," Mrs. Williams went

71

on. "It says that if it turns out to be true, then Llanfair will have the better claim to the name of Beddgelert than the town that has called itself that since the Middle Ages. That will show those snooty folk down in the valley, won't it now?"

"I think we'll have to wait and see," Evan said with a smile. "Personally I think that everyone's hoping for too much from this. There are saints' tombs and chapels all over Wales. And nobody's even heard of Saint Celert."

"It gives us something to be proud of though, doesn't it?" Mrs. Williams went on. "Until now Llanfair was just a few farms and a village where the slate workers lived. Since the mine closed, it's had nothing. Of course, if they open the mine again, the way they're talking of doing, then who knows? Any way you look at it, it's a great day for Llanfair, and the meeting tonight should be very exciting."

"Not too exciting, we hope," Even said as he sat down to his breakfast.

"Let's just hope they don't bring the poor old colonel's body back here today," Mrs. Williams went on. "We could never have the meeting with him lying in state in the chapel next door, could we?"

"I shouldn't think it's likely he'll be buried here," Evan said. "His home was in London, after all. He's probably made funeral arrangements for himself down there."

"More's the pity," Mrs. Williams said. "He loved these mountains."

"He certainly did," Evan agreed. He thought of the colonel, currently lying in a drawer in the police morgue. He didn't know whether to hope that the pathologist would find suspicious circumstances or not. The old boy deserved a dignified funeral and the chance to rest in peace. But if he had been murdered, Evan definitely wanted to make sure that someone didn't get away with it.

Mrs. Williams was obviously still in her mourning mode because breakfast was only toast that had been sitting for some time, getting cold in the toast rack. Evan ate a couple of slices and then made his way down the street to the police station. He had only gone a few yards when the milk float pulled up beside him and Evans-the-Milk leaned out.

"Have you seen what that bloody fool's gone and done now then, eh, Evan bach?" he yelled.

"Who's gone and done what?" Evan asked warily. Not another body in the river, he prayed.

"That hothead next door," Evans-the-Milk said, nodding his head in the direction of the butcher's shop. "Have you seen the paper yet? It was him. He was down in Caernarfon yesterday and he hears that a reporter from the *Daily Post* is in the bar. So he goes over to him and tells him that he's got a scoop for him. He must have spun that journalist a good yarn too, because it made the front page." He climbed down with three milk bottles in his hand and put them on a doorstep. "I just hope we don't look stupid when the archaeologists go and take a look at the site," he said, straightening up again. "And all that stuff about changing our name and going for the new record of the longest name in the world—we haven't even decided anything yet, have we?"

"The meeting's tonight," Evan agreed.

"He's got a screw loose, that man," Evans-the-Milk went on. "I knew he was a raging nationalist, but I didn't realize it went as far as doing anything to make Llanfair famous. I mean, what does it matter if we've got a saint's tomb or not?"

"Just don't say that to Evans-the-Meat or he'll be after you with the meat chopper." Evan chuckled.

"What I can't see is this," Evans-the-Milk said, climbing back into the milk float. "He wants Llanfair to be famous and to hold world records, but he doesn't want any tourists to come here to see it. Doesn't that sound to you like a screw loose?"

"He won't be able to stop the tourists after this," Evan said. "Even the column in the paper will bring them, won't it?"

"Of course it will," Evans-the-Milk called back from his driver's seat. "So I'd better get cracking with my homemade ice cream, hadn't I? What do you think about blackberry for a flavor? My wife makes lovely blackberry jam. I thought I could use that."

The milk float took off with the low hum of its electric motor, leaving Evan shaking his head.

He put his key in the door of his little office that grandly called itself Llanfair District Community Police Substation, and went inside. There was no message from Sargeant Watkins and Evan hesitated to call. The pathologist might have shown up late to work after an exhausting fishing trip. He put the kettle on for his morning cup of tea and settled down to his paperwork.

It was just after ten when the phone rang.

"Okay, Evan boy, so you were right again." Sergeant Watkin's voice echoed down the line.

"The autopsy's been done?" Evan asked.

"Yeah, and he didn't die by drowning. The old boy was dead by the time he hit the water. No water in the lungs. The D.I. wants me to come right over and report back to him if I think we're dealing with a murder."

"Does he think the colonel might have clubbed himself to death?"

"No, but it's just possible that he fell onto a rock, hit his head, and then slid into the water later."

"Hit his head and then slid into the water later? Have you seen how the water flows over those rocks? He'd have been swept away before he was dead and there would be water in his lungs."

"You're probably right, but D.I. Hughes doesn't particularly want another murder on his hands right now. He'd like to get some fishing in this summer."

"You'd better spread the word to the criminal population,"

74

Evan said dryly. "No more activity until the D.I. has caught a big one."

Watkins chuckled. "I'll be right over," he said. "I'm bringing a couple of chaps from forensic with me, but play it down in the village, will you? Let them go on thinking it's an accident. We don't want to scare anyone unnecessarily."

"And we don't want to alert the murderer that we're onto him," Evan added.

"If it turns out to be murder," Watkins said.

Half an hour later the white police van pulled up beside the bridge. Sergeant Watkins got out, followed by two serious-looking young men in raincoats. The clouds had come back that morning and it was threatening to rain any minute.

"I'm glad you got here," Evan said, shaking Watkins' hand. "I was worried the rain would wash away any evidence there might be."

Together they ducked under the tape and walked along the riverbank.

"Exactly where was he lying when you found him?" Watkins asked.

Evan pointed to a spot about ten yards below the bridge. The river here no longer fell steeply over rocks, but flowed steadily, two or three feet deep, over pebbles and water weed. Watkins nodded. "If he'd fallen off the bridge, he'd have probably wound up here, given the force of water above," he said.

Evan was examining the bank where they were now standing. "Look at this, sarge," he said. "Someone has been here."

The riverbank at this point was a riot of grass, wild flowers, and shrubs. Evan indicated a bare patch among the grass. "Someone has pulled up some plants here, and it looks like they've dug up the soil too," he said.

"Why would they do that?"

"I'd guess there might have been some blood on the ground, or maybe the plants were flattened where the body fell."

Watkins stared at the ground for a while. "It could also be dogs burying bones or wild pigs digging for roots, or even kiddies playing with mud pies," he said.

"But it wasn't like this on Saturday," Evan insisted. "I would have noticed it."

"I'll ask the boys to take samples."

"Have them take samples here too," Evan said, pointing between tall rye grasses. "There's blood here."

"Where?" Watkins squatted and parted the grass with his pen, disturbing several big flies that rose, buzzing indignantly.

"You can't see it any more, because it's been cleared away, but the flies know," Evan said. "They can detect the smallest trace of blood. See how they were all congregated here and not anywhere else? I bet they could smell blood."

"Okay, Sherlock Holmes, so what was used as the murder weapon?" Watkins demanded.

"That's pretty obvious," Evan said. "There are plenty of them still lying here." The river's edge was full of smooth, fist-sized rocks. "It would be the easiest thing in the world to choose a rock, lie in wait, then bam. He falls and you throw the rock back in the river where all the blood gets washed away."

Watkins nodded agreement. "So the big question is why anyone would want to lie in wait and hit him over the head."

"I've asked a few tactful questions around the village," Evan said, "and frankly I'm stumped."

"I'm glad to hear that for once," Watkins said. "I thought you were about to tell me that you'd solved the case single handed. He was a millionaire and his disgruntled nephew had been waiting for this chance."

"It's possible," Evan said. "We don't know much about his life in London, but we do know he didn't have much cash. His clothes were very well worn."

"So? Lots of millionaires are eccentric misers."

Evan shook his head. "I don't think that applies to the colonel. He was a generous man by nature, always buying drinks for people. I think he was genuinely living on a small pension."

"So what's your theory?"

Evan stared past the police sergeant, his eyes following the path back to the pub. "Unless it was a madman waiting to clobber the first person who went by, then it had to be someone who knew the colonel's habits," he said. "The person who did this knew that the colonel took this shortcut from the pub every night."

"A local then?"

"Except that I've talked to several people who were in the pub that night and between us we can account for most of the men in the village. The ones who weren't there were good family men, home with the kiddies, or a couple of lads out at the pictures in Caernarfon."

"That makes it an outsider, or a woman," Watkins commented. "But as you said, it would have been a pretty strong woman."

Evan nodded. "I got him out of the river. He was damned heavy. I don't think a woman could have dragged him any distance alone. And anyway, do women go around hitting people over the head?"

"If they're desperate enough," Watkins said, "and it's the only way out. But what about a motive? No little feud the colonel had with anybody here? No complaints about loud music or telling young blokes to get their hair cut?"

"Nothing like that," Evan said. "The only thing really that happened before he died was that he found this ruin up on the hill."

"Oh yes," Watkins said. "I've been reading about it in the paper. Quite an important find, I understand."

"If it's really what they think it is," Evan said. "They've still got to have the archaeologists from the university take a look at it."

"You say he discovered it?"

"Yes, a couple of hours before he died. He came rushing into the pub, all excited, and we all went up there with him to take a look for ourselves. Then we came back, he gulped down another Scotch, and left in a hurry."

"Why did he do that?"

"It was odd, really. He started telling me this story about seeing someone he recognized and then he switched stories to an absurd tale about someone breaking his neck playing polo. He was definitely rattled."

"You think he'd just seen someone he recognized from somewhere else?"

"Except that they were all locals in the pub and what's more they all stayed in the pub when he left. We accounted for them all being there after he'd gone. It's possible he ran into someone he knew earlier in the day, I suppose, but then why was he suddenly uncomfortable about telling the story?"

"Doesn't make sense, does it," Watkins said. "I mean, even if he'd seen someone he recognized from somewhere else, it doesn't follow that the person was out to kill him. Who'd want to kill an old man like that? Even if you had a grudge against him, you'd know he'd be dead in a couple of years."

"And I can't imagine why anyone would have a grudge against the colonel," Evan said. "As I said, everyone here was fond of him. They thought he was a funny old boffer and laughed about him, but in a good-natured way—no malice in it."

"There was plenty of malice in hitting him over the head and shoving him into the river," Watkins observed. "Where was he staying? You'd better take me to talk to his landlady."

"Up there at Owens' farm." Evan indicated the square gray stone building on the hill above them. "I spoke to her on Saturday and she couldn't really tell me anything. It didn't seem that the colonel had any contact with the outside world while he was here. No phone calls or letters, no strangers coming to visit. You might get more out of her than I did. She was so upset that she kept breaking off to blow her nose when I was there."

"We better go and talk to her anyway," Sergeant Watkins said. "You know what D.I. Hughes is like. He'll chew me out if I tell him that you'd been interviewing people on my behalf."

"Then what's the next step, sarge?" Evan asked as they crossed the bridge together and headed for Owens' farm.

"I expect the D.I. will want to take a look for himself and when the lab results from the site samples come in, we'll look into his will and next of kin. Then he'll probably get in touch with the Metropolitan Police in London and have them get us the details of his life down there. Hughes is not going to be happy about this. Damn."

"I'm not very happy about it myself," Evan said. "I really liked the old boy. I want his murderer caught. I'd like to help in any way I can."

"You're in a better position than anyone to keep your eyes and ears open around here," Sergeant Watkins said. "If his killer is a local man, then something's going to come out. One good thing about murderers is that they can never keep the murder to themselves. In the end the suspense is going to be so great that he'll say or do something to give himself away. He might come forward and volunteer to help you with your enquiries. Keep close tabs on anyone who seems particularly interested in the case."

"Righto, sarge. So do you want me to let on that we suspect it's murder?"

"It will have to come out the moment the D.I. gets here. But until then, stay mum. It might rattle our killer into coming to ask us questions if he's not sure how much we know."

"As long as it doesn't rattle him into killing someone else," Evan pointed out. "We've got a big meeting in the village tonight to discuss what we're going to do about this ruin."

"Going to do about the ruin?" Sergeant Watkins looked amused.

Evan grinned too. "Yes, they've got crazy ideas about changing the village's name and God knows what else."

"You'll be there?"

"I'll have to. Things might get pretty lively."

"Good. Who knows, something might come out of it— some kind of motive, maybe."

"Like what?"

"I've no idea at the moment. But see who shows special interest in this ruin."

"It doesn't make sense to me," Evan said. "If someone hadn't wanted the colonel to find the ruin, it was pretty senseless to kill him after he'd told the whole world about it. And anyway, why would someone want the ruin not to be found? It's only a few old rocks."

Sergeant Watkins patted Evan on the back. "That's for you to find out, Sherlock."

Chapter 9

The village hall was a rickety wooden building with a corrugated iron roof. It stood behind Chapel Bethel and was the only structure in the village that looked temporary, although it had actually been in place since 1941. It was packed to capacity by the time Evan arrived on Monday evening. All the chairs were occupied and people lined the walls. Evan squeezed in close to the door.

"They certainly don't get this kind of turnout on election day," he commented to Mrs. Williams, who had come with him. "I'd no idea there were this many people in the village. I've never even seen some of them before."

"There's a lot of strangers here," Mrs. Williams said, after scrutinizing the crowd. "I shouldn't be surprised if there aren't reporters here and we'll make the front page in the newspaper again tomorrow. Maybe we'll even be on the telly." She pushed her way forward and perched half of her large seat on a chair in the front row already occupied by Mary Hopkins.

The reverend Parry Davies climbed onto a small raised platform at one end of the hall. An expectant hush fell over the packed room.

"Welcome every one of you," he said in the booming voice

that had won him first place in several eisteddfods. " 'Deed to goodness, this is a historic moment in the long history of Llanfair. As you all know by now, this meeting has been called to discuss the momentous discovery made by Colonel Arbuthnot on Friday last. But before we start, I'd like us to stand in a moment of silent prayer in memory of the colonel, who died tragically so soon after his moment of triumph."

Chairs scraped as over a hundred people rose to their feet. Evan's gaze swept the room as they stood, heads bowed. But he noticed no signs of guilty behavior, no one shifting uncomfortably or glancing around nervously. If the murderer was here, then he was cool and confident enough not to give himself away. Evan shook his head. What a ridiculous idea—to think that someone from this village, people he had known for over a year now, might be involved in a murder.

Chairs scraped again as the minute of silence ended and an undercurrent of excited conversation went around the room until Mr. Parry Davies raised his hand and spoke again. "As you have undoubtedly all heard, the colonel found what he thought might be King Arthur's fort, up above the village. Several members of the village, including myself, went to examine his discovery. On observing the shape and size of the ruin, I determined that this was too small to be anything but a chapel. This had to be what we have all believed to exist, but never been able to find—the true resting place of Saint Celert. The real, the true Beddgelert! Not some trumped up legend of a dog's grave but the final resting place of a saint!"

There was mumbling from the audience, but Mr. Parry Davies raised his hand again and went on loudly. "I have been in touch with the archaeology department at Bangor University, and they have assured me that they will be sending out experts to verify our find at the earliest possible opportunity. If they confirm what we suspect, and I have every hope that they will, then it will be a proud day for Llanfair. Llanfair will then be the true Beddgelert."

A man sitting a few rows from the back tried to stand up but was restrained by the people on either side of him. On one side of the podium, Evans-the-Meat attempted to catch Rev. Parry Davies' attention. The minister saw him and cleared his throat, a trifle nervously.

"Our local butcher, Mr. Gareth Evans, has asked to be given the floor at this point. So I turn the meeting over to him."

Evans-the-Meat leaped onto the stage. He looked quite different without his bloodstained apron. In a dark suit, with his hair slicked down, he came across as a person of substance and authority. "Fellow citizens of Llanfair," he said grandly. "This is indeed a proud moment for us. All these years we've had to sit by and watch while other villages glorified in the great history of Wales. We've never had an eisteddfod, we've never been able to celebrate great battles or even legends from our Celtic past. But now we have the true resting place of Saint Celert, and I'm sure you join with me in wanting the rest of Wales to know about it. I therefore propose that we let the world know of our great discovery by changing our name officially to Llanfairbeddgelert."

There was scattered applause and a few rowdy cheers from Barry-the-Bucket and his friends, who had already been in the Dragon since opening time. But the cheers were interrupted by a man who jumped to his feet, shaking off the people who tried to restrain him. "How dare you!" he yelled. "Don't think you're going to get away with this, because we'll fight you every step of the way. Think you'll change your name to Llanfairbeddgelert, is it now?" He fought his way forward and came down the aisle. He was a large man in a tweed jacket. His heavily jowled face was almost purple with rage, and his jowls quivered as his head shook. "Let me tell you that there already is a place that has rejoiced in the name of Beddgelert since before the village of Llanfair was even thought of. We've been the one and only Beddgelert for hundreds of years, and what's more, we're going to stay the one and only Beddgelert. We're proud of our town and we're proud of Gelert's grave and we'll stop this insanity any way we can. Go ahead and you'll be facing us in court!"

"Sit down! Shut up!" The protests grew around the room. Evan was about to take a step forward to prevent trouble when the big man spun around.

"I've said what I came to say," he yelled. "I hope that most people here are sensible enough not to go along with this damned-fool idea because if this goes to court, I'll bankrupt you all."

He glared at the audience, then suddenly frowned and looked around as if he was no longer sure where he was. He shoved his way down the center aisle and hurried out. There was silence followed by nervous laughter.

"Don't listen to him," Evans-the-Meat yelled after him. "Idle threats—that's what it is. He's just hot air. Thinks we'll take away his precious tourist trade, isn't it? Well, I tell him he's welcome to his tourists. Keep them down there in the valley, but let us glory in our heritage!"

More polite applause.

"And while we're on the subject of changing our name," Evans-the-Meat went on, "I say let's go the whole hog. We won't just stop with Llanfairbeddgelert. Why not call ourselves Llanfairbeddgelert-who-was-not-a-dog-but-a-saint-and-who-had-his-chapel-up-on-the-mountain-at-the-top-of-the-pass-above-the-larch-trees-and-near-the-big-rocks . . ." Laughter drowned out the rest of his sentence.

"They don't make postcards big enough, man!" someone yelled from the back.

Evans-the-Meat flushed a little then held up his hand for quiet. "You see what I'm suggesting, don't you? Think about that other village called Llanfair over on Anglesey. What does it have that we don't have? Nothing, except the longest name in the world. Everyone has heard of that Llanfair and nobody has heard of us, only because of the length of their name. So I

84

say let's put our Llanfair on the map. Let's give ourselves a name that is one syllable longer than theirs and we'll find ourselves in the Guinness book of records instead of them!"

Several people near the front had risen to their feet. A distinguished-looking man strode to the podium. "I am mayor of the town of Llanfairpwllgwyngyllgogerychwyrndrobwllllantysiliogogogoch!" he announced proudly. "We read in the paper that you people up here were thinking of doing this unspeakable thing. I am here to tell you what the representative from Beddgelert has already told you. Do this and we will take legal action to put a stop to it!"

"There's nothing to stop us, man, and you know it!" Evans-the-Meat yelled back. His face was now beet red. "We can call ourselves what we like."

"Not when we are the true owners of the longest name in the world," the man went on.

"Longest name in the world? Hah!" Evans-the-Meat roared. "And when did you acquire this longest name in the world? Only when you got a railway station and you wanted something impressive to put on the sign."

"That's not true!" the man started, but Evans-the-Meat cut in.

"My great-auntie Mwfanwy came from Anglesey and she remembers that your village was just known as plain old Llanfair until the railway got there."

"Been alive for a hundred and fifty years, has she then?" one of the other Llanfair P.G. delegation demanded. "That's how long we've had the railway. And we had our long name before that. We just didn't care to use it officially in those days. It took too long to write."

"There was probably nobody who knew how to write in your village anyway," a voice jeered from the back of the hall.

"Order! Order!" The reverend Parry Davies thumped on the podium.

"It doesn't matter how long we've had our name," the

85

mayor went on. "It's ours and we're proud of it. Go ahead with this ridiculous publicity stunt and you'll have not one but two lawsuits on your hands. I hope you all have deep pockets here because lawyers don't come cheap." He turned to those with him. "Come on, boys, we've said all that we came to say. Let's leave these folk to come to their senses!"

With that he swept out of the hall, followed by his retinue.

"Anyone else who's got something to say?" Barry-the-Bucket's voice cut through the murmurs. "Is Saint Celert here, maybe, wanting to tell us that it's not his grave after all?"

Through the noisy outbursts that followed, the reverend Parry Davies mounted the podium again. "Please, please," he begged. "Ladies and gentlemen." The noise gradually subsided. "In the light of what has just occurred, I think it might be prudent to postpone any more discussion to another occasion. It also might be wise to contact a solicitor at this juncture and get his advice before hurtling ourselves headlong into the abyss. I'm sure I speak for everyone here when I say that I have no wish to be part of any unpleasant court proceedings."

"They don't scare me one bit," Evans-the-Meat said loudly. "Let them just try it. We'll make them look like the fools they are."

"But, Mr. Evans," the minister went on, "think of Christian charity. Love thy neighbor—that's what we are instructed to do. If this is so abhorrent to our neighbors, have we a right to proceed with it?"

"They can go to hell as far as I'm concerned," Evans-the-Meat retorted. "Let them go ahead and be damned."

"There will be no damning while I'm in the room," Mr. Parry Davies said firmly. "I strongly advise that we break up this meeting until tempers have cooled and we have had time to examine the ramifications."

A thin figure in black rose to his feet. "I completely concur with my learned colleague," Reverend Powell-Jones said, turning to address the audience.

"That makes a first," a voice commented in a loud stage whisper. "They never agree on anything."

"So shall we close up the meeting for tonight then?" Rev. Parry Davies asked the assembly.

"Hold on a moment. I've got something to say." Ted Morgan stepped up onto the platform. In contrast to the previous speakers, he wasn't wearing a jacket, but a light blue golf shirt over well cut slacks. The hall was instantly quiet. "Before everyone leaves, I have an announcement to make. Most of you already know who I am." Ted looked around the audience with a self-satisfied smile on his face. "For those of you who haven't been in the Dragon and had a chance to meet me yet, I'm old Taff Morgan's son. I've been living in London for most of my adult life and I've done pretty well at it too. Now I've decided to give it a try back where I started. Some of you have probably heard—most of you, if I know the village grapevine—that I've bought the old slate quarry." There was a stir of excitement in the audience. "It's quite true. I bought it a few months ago and now I'm at liberty to tell you what I plan to do with it." He reached into his pants pocket and produced an envelope. "This came today to say that planning permission has been granted."

"Planning permission for what?" a voice demanded.

Ted stepped closer to his audience. "Those of you who worked in the old mine will remember that it is a dramatic and beautiful place—vast slate caverns, an underground lake. What a shame to keep it all shut away. It's the sort of place that's crying out to be revived. That's why I decided to set my adventure park there. I'm going to create a theme park called The Haunted Mine. Doesn't it just lend itself to that kind of thing? Picture a ghost train ride going through the little tunnels with spooks jumping out around every corner, a roller coaster in the main cavern, a waterslide coming into the lake. Pretty powerful stuff, eh? And the whole thing will be linked by monorail to a big new hotel I'm going to build on the old farm."

Evans-the-Meat leaped at him. "Are you out of your mind, man?" he screamed. "The Haunted Mine? A monorail? A big hotel? The place crawling with tourists? Over my dead body!"

"Easy now, Gareth boy," Ted Morgan said with a laugh. "It will be good for Llanfair. Think of the jobs. Think of all that cash waiting to be spent here. You want this place put on the map? I'll put in on for you."

"Not with your damned sleazy commercial ideas, you won't," Evans-the-Meat yelled. "You never did appreciate what we've got here and now you're going to wreck it for us."

"You can't stop me." Ted Morgan chuckled. "I told you. I've already got the go-ahead from the Gwyneth County Council and the Welsh tourism board. They're even thinking of giving me a grant to get it started. They said it was badly needed in a depressed area like Llanfair."

"Depressed area?" Evans-the-Meat shouted.

"Full of backward-thinking half wits like you, boy," Ted Morgan jeered.

Evans-the-Meat uttered an enraged roar and flung himself at Ted. Evan had been standing alert and poised at the back of the hall. He ran forward to prise Evans-the-Meat's hands from Ted's throat. Barrry-the-Bucket and several of his friends rushed to join Evan in pulling apart the two men.

"Easy now, man, unless you want to spend the night in jail," Evan said softly. Evans-the-Meat still struggled. "Let me get at him. I'll kill him first," he yelled as he was half carried, half dragged down the center aisle. "I'll kill him, I swear it. We all said good riddance when he went away and nobody wants him back again now."

Evan noticed that the butcher smelled strongly of beer. So he had been getting up his courage before the meeting started. They dragged him into the cool night air.

"What shall we do with him?" Barry's friend asked Evan.

"Let go of me. I'll teach that slimy little snake Morgan a lesson he won't forget," Evans-the-Meat threatened.

"Do you want to spend a night in a cell?" Evan demanded. "I don't want to call for a squad car, but I will unless you calm down and stop talking so daft."

Evans-the-Meat gradually stopped struggling. "You don't know him," he growled. "He's no good for this place. Never was, never will be. Nothing but trouble."

"It seems like you're the one who's causing all the trouble right now," Evan said. "We're going to walk you home and I suggest that you go straight to bed."

It had started to rain, a sudden, stinging shower that seemed to sober up Evans-the-Meat by the time they reached his front door. His living quarters were in a flat over the butcher shop.

"Is your wife home?" Evan asked as he fumbled with his key.

"Visiting her mother in Dolgellau again," Evans-the-Meat said. "She's always visiting her mother in Dolgellau."

"I can trust you to stay home and go to bed, can't I?" Evan demanded. "I don't want to find you've gone to the pub and caused more trouble."

"I won't go to the pub," Evans-the-Meat said with a little sigh. "I'll be a good boy, officer. I've got a lot of thinking to do."

"Alright then," Evan said, hesitating as Evans-the-Meat began to close the door. He stood in the street outside.

"We'll be off then, if you don't need us any more." Barry-the-Bucket put his hand on Evan's shoulder.

"Oh, right. Thanks for your help," Evan said, shaking hands with him. "I think everything will be alright now."

The sound of voices echoed down the street. It was apparent that the meeting had already broken up and groups of people were coming toward them, oblivious of the rain, chatting excitedly about the events that had just taken place. Mrs. Williams saw Evan and came scurrying over to join him, her face alight and eyes shining.

89

"Who would have thought it, Mr. Evans? We haven't seen this much excitement here since that German bomber lost its way and crashed on Mount Snowdon during the war. A proper old ruckus, wasn't it? All that shoutin' and carryin' on." She glanced around conspiratorially. "Did you manage to get Evans-the-Meat calmed down then?"

"Eventually," Evan said. "He's a strong bloke. It took four of us."

Mrs. Williams shook her head, making little clucking noises. "He always did have a terrible temper, that one." She looked up and down the street. "Are you coming home now then?"

"I'd better stay out here for a while," Evan said, "just to make sure there's no more upsets tonight. But you should go home. The rain's coming down harder now."

"You'll get soaked to your skin. Shall I pop home and get you your raincoat?"

"I'll be fine, thanks. I'll see you in a little while." Evan had to smile. Sometimes Mrs. Williams made him feel that he was five years old again and just setting off for primary school. He watched her hurry on down the street and disappear into the darkness beyond the street lamp. Then he turned up his collar against the driving rain and walked slowly back up the length of the village. The village hall was also in darkness now and he met Mr. Parry Davies coming down the path toward him.

"I sent them all home, constable," he said. "I thought there was no point in prolonging things at this point."

"Quite right, reverend. I'm glad you did," Evan said. "We've had enough hot temper for one night."

He looked up as he heard a car start and drive away with tires squealing.

"I'll be off home then," the reverend Parry Davies said. "I'm glad you were there, Constable Evans. A tricky situation, wasn't it just?"

90

"I've seen worse," Evan said. "But it was too much excitement in one night."

The reverend chuckled as he opened his gate. Evan patrolled slowly back down the street. It was now deserted, and strips of light were all that showed between tightly drawn curtains as the inhabitants of Llanfair were safely back in their living rooms with the telly on. He paused again outside the butcher shop and looked up at the lighted window upstairs. There was nothing more he could do. He hoped that Evans-the-Meat would have the sense to have cooled off by morning.

Mrs. Williams must have been watching and waiting for him to come home because the front door opened before he could put his key in the lock.

"Any more signs of trouble?" she asked, half expectantly.

Evan shook head. "Everyone's gone home."

She helped him off with his wet jacket. "Look at you, soaked to the skin just. Come and sit in the kitchen and I'll make you a nice hot cocoa."

"I'm fine, Mrs. Williams," Evan protested. "A spot of rain won't hurt me." He glanced at his reflection the hall mirror. "Quite a night, wasn't it? I always knew that Evans-the-Meat got upset easily, but I wasn't prepared for that."

Mrs. Williams shook her head. "Shocking," she said. "Of course, there's always been bad blood between those two."

"Evans-the-Meat and Ted Morgan, you mean?" Evan asked with interest.

Mrs. Williams nodded furiously. "Oh yes, 'deed to goodness. They never could abide each other, even back in primary school here. The number of canings they got for fighting—I should think their backsides were black and blue all over! Ted Morgan always seemed to know how to get Evans-the-Meat riled up and make him lose his temper. Always teasing him, he was, and that boy had a terrible temper, even back in those days." She leaned closer to Evan, as if she was afraid someone might overhear them. "He went for a boy called Tommy Hughes for laughing at him once and landed him in the hospital with a broken jaw."

"Then Ted Morgan should be grateful that I stepped in just in time," Evan commented.

He followed Mrs. Williams into the kitchen and watched as she put a kettle on the stove. "There were some pretty hot tempers in that room. That man from Beddgelert was as bad as Evans-the-Meat. I thought he was going to break a blood vessel the way he was yelling."

"That's Mr. Dawson who runs the Royal Stag Hotel," Mrs. Williams confided. "You know, that big fancy hotel just across the bridge with the ivy on it?"

Evan nodded. "No wonder he was so upset at the thought of tourism being taken away from Beddgelert."

"He never used to be like that," Mrs. Williams said as she got two cups down from the dresser. "I suppose you can understand how he got that way, after the tragedy he's known, poor man."

"What happened?"

Mrs. Williams shook her head sadly, making more clucking noises. "His daughter killed herself," she whispered, although they were quite alone. "They only had the one child and he idolized her. She was a pretty little thing too. Well, maybe he tried to protect her a little too much, maybe he was just too strict with her, because she ran away and got in with a bad crowd. They say she got involved in drugs and ended up taking her own life." She started ladling cocoa into the cups. "He took it very hard. And then his wife couldn't stand it any longer and she up and left him. Afterward he was a changed man—always picking fights with people and yelling."

Evan pulled out a chair. "Evans-the-Meat's always picking fights and he doesn't even have an excuse," he commented. "I just hope he simmers down, although I can't see that he'll ever go along with this new idea of Ted Morgan's."

92

"What do you think of it then, Mr. Evans?"

"It doesn't sound like a bad idea to me," Evan said cautiously. "It would mean lots of jobs, wouldn't it, and it would make use of something that's lying idle right now. I'm not sure that I'd like a big hotel and a monorail right here in the village, but I suppose these things can be done tastefully."

"I don't know that I'd like all that traffic and people peering in my windows," Mrs. Williams said, "but you can't stop progress, can you. Are you hungry now, Mr. Evans?" She looked around the kitchen for inspiration. "Can I make you a nice cheese sandwich? Or how about cold bacon pie and pickles? Or some of my eccles cakes?"

Evan was spared from answering these questions by the phone ringing in the front hall.

"Now who could that be at this time of night?" Mrs. Williams demanded as she always did when the phone rang. Evan wasn't sure how she expected him to be clairvoyant and know.

He went to pick it up. "Hello? Williams residence. Constable Evans speaking."

"Mr. Evans? This is Annie. Annie Pigeon," a voice whispered. "I think someone's trying to break into my house."

Chapter 10

The rain had stopped as Evan hurried out of the house. The street was deserted and the faint sound of dramatic music punctuated with explosions came from TV sets behind heavy curtains. The pavement glistened in the street light but there was a large patch of shadow before the next light up by the school. Wisps of cloud hung like ghostly shadows on the slopes above. Evan's feet echoed from the stone walls as he broke into a run.

Annie must have been watching for him because she opened the front door before he reached her cottage. She wasn't wearing makeup this time, and her face looked deathly white against her red hair. She was dressed in old dark sweats and Evan wondered if she had already undressed for bed. Her eyes darted nervously around as she let him into the narrow hallway.

"What happened then?" he asked.

Annie glanced toward the back door and then up the stairs. "I think he might still be there," she whispered. "I didn't dare go into the kitchen, because I thought I could see the glow of a cigarette."

"Stay there," Evan said. He went down the hall and into

the tiny kitchen without turning on the kitchen light. The back door was shut. So was the kitchen window. Without hesitating he crossed to the back door and wrenched it open.

"Alright, what's going on out here?" he demanded.

Silence. His flashlight strafed the little back garden and the bushes beyond. He waited, holding his breath but there was no sound, only the sigh of the wind. A concrete path led to the back fence with flower beds on either side of it. He walked down the path, examining the beds for footprints. Of course an intruder need never have stepped off the path to reach her kitchen. There was a rickety back gate that wasn't properly latched. Someone might have gone out that way. He opened it and shone his flashlight along the footpath in both directions but there was no sign of movement except for branches swaying in the wind.

"Did you see him?" Annie's anxious voice asked as he headed back into the house.

Evan shook his head. He shone the light over the window and door frame. The paint was peeling on both but there was no sign of recent interference.

"Tell me what happened," he said as he went inside and shut the door behind him.

"I was upstairs, putting my Jenny to bed," Annie said, still talking in whispers. "I heard people go past talking and then it got quiet. I went into the back bedroom where I sleep to get something and I just happened to glance out of the window and I thought I saw a shadow streak across my back garden toward the house. And then I heard this scratching sound, like someone trying to get in. I tiptoed downstairs and I could see his cigarette. He was standing there in the dark."

"Any idea who it was?" Evan peered out of the window again.

She shook her head.

Evan went over to the window, then he turned back to her with a grin. "Are you sure you didn't mistake this for a cigarette?" he asked, pointing to the little red light that glowed on the electric stove. It was reflected in the window glass.

Annie bit her lip. "Oh, I see," she said. "Yeah, I might have done. I was that scared."

"The wind does strange things up here," Evan said kindly. "You might have heard a branch scraping on something and the trees moving in the street light can throw strange shadows."

She nodded, still wide-eyed. "You may be right," she said. "Perhaps my imagination is getting the better of me, except . . ."

"Except what?"

She looked away. "It almost sounds daft to say it now, but I suspected someone had been here yesterday. You know when we were out up on the hill? When I got back the kitchen window was open and I'd swear I closed it before we left. I looked around and it didn't seem as if anything had been taken, but I just got the feeling that someone had been snooping around and hadn't put things back how I left them."

She led him out of the darkened kitchen into a sparsely furnished living room. There was a green vinyl armchair, a bean bag, and a clothes basket full of toys. A small TV sat on top of a bookcase that held a few children's books.

"It wasn't robbery, was it?" he said. "Or they would have taken the TV. You've no idea why anybody would want to get into your house?"

She shook her head. "No idea at all."

Evan looked directly at her. "You don't think someone might have found out where you were living? Someone who might have been looking for you and followed you here?"

He thought she hesitated before she said, "Nobody at all. Jenny and me have no one. We're all alone."

"I see," he said, but he didn't see. He found himself wondering if this was a ruse to get him round to her house for an evening visit. That's what Mrs. Williams would have suspected.

Bronwen too. But Annie was clearly upset. Her eyes darted around nervously and she was playing with the ring she wore on her right hand.

"Mummy! Where are you? I want you up here." Jenny's voice wailed.

"I better go up to her," Annie said. "Poor little kid. She could tell I was scared. I tried not to let her see, but she could tell." She headed for the stairs. "I won't be a moment, I hope. Then maybe you'd like a glass of wine or something? I've got a bottle of Spanish plonk."

Without waiting for him to answer she ran upstairs. Evan went on standing in the living room, unsure whether it might be wiser to go home now. She'd have to file an official report, of course, but she could do that in the morning. He looked around a little, wondering what an intruder could possibly have wanted in here. He pulled back the curtains and looked out onto the street. Then he went through to the kitchen and examined the back of the house again. The fences were low and anyone could have easily come and gone via a neighboring back garden—but why, if nothing had been taken. Unless Annie wasn't telling him the whole truth.

"I'll never get her to sleep now." Annie came up behind him without his hearing her. "She's scared of burglars getting into her room." She looked up at him, her eyes pleading. "I wonder if you'd go up and say goodnight to her. It might reassure her to know that a policeman is here."

"Alright, if you think it will help."

"I'd be ever so grateful," Annie said, leading the way upstairs. Jenny's room was also sparsely furnished except for a shelf full of dolls and stuffed animals, but her bedspread had a pretty animal quilt on it and there was a Noah's ark lamp on her bedside table. It was clear that Annie put any money she had into her daughter. Jenny looked up at Evan with big scared eyes. He thought he must look like a giant to her in that tiny room.

"Hello, Jenny. Your mum wanted me to come and tell you that I've checked the house and everything is quite safe," he said.

"So you see, love, you've nothing to be scared of," Annie said. "Why don't you shut your eyes and go to sleep now. I tell you what—would you like Mr. Evans to read you a bedtime story?" She turned to Evan. "She loves stories. You can read to her for hours and she never gets tired of it. Would you mind?"

Evan didn't feel that he had much choice. "I don't know if I'm good at reading stories," he said. "I haven't had much practice."

"I'm sure Jenny would love it," Annie said. "Here, this is her favorite." She picked up a book and handed it to him.

"Not that one, *The Three Bad Monkeys*," Jenny said, sitting up suddenly animated.

"But you like this one," Annie said. "It was your favorite last week."

"This week I like the *Three Bad Monkeys*," Jenny said.

Annie looked around. "I don't know where the monkey book is right now. How about we settle for this one, okay?"

"Okay," Jenny said, lying back again.

"Go on, sit down," Annie instructed Evan. "Make yourself comfortable. I'll go down and see if I can find that bottle of wine and a corkscrew."

Evan opened *Puss in Boots*. From what he could remember it was a gruesome story and not what you'd want to read to a nervous child late at night.

Jenny sat up, wanting to see all the pictures as he read the story and offering her own comments on each page. "Look, he doesn't have any clothes on! See—that's the bad ogre. He eats people."

It took a long time to get through the book and when he had finished Jenny begged him to read another one. Evan looked around but there was no sign of Annie.

"I expect your mum wants you to go to sleep now," he said.

"Just one more story first," Jenny said.

"Okay. Just one, then you must promise to shut your eyes and go to sleep."

"Alright." Jenny gave him a sweet smile.

He read a book about a puppy's busy day, and Jenny's eyes were nodding shut by the time he had finished. He got up quietly and switched off the bedside light before tiptoeing down the stairs. He met Annie just about to come up the stairs with a glass in her hands.

"Oh, you gave me a turn." She gasped as she suddenly caught sight of him.

"She's asleep," Evan whispered. "I was creeping."

"I found the wine. Then I thought I'd leave you two to it," Annie said. "To give you a chance to get to know each other."

Evan decided that his suspicions might well have been correct. It was just possible that Annie had made up an excuse to get him here. Was she also trying to win him over by using Jenny?

"I really ought to be getting back," he said as she held out the wine glass to him. "We'll have to file an official report on your prowler, but we can do that down at the station in the morning."

"What's the hurry?" Annie asked. "You can sit and have a glass of wine with me, can't you? I need a chance to get my nerves calmed down."

Evan noticed that her hand was trembling as she handed him the glass and he felt ashamed of thinking that she might have lured him here under false pretenses. He took the glass she was offering. "Where's yours?" he asked.

"On the kitchen table." She led him through to the kitchen.

Again he was struck by its bleakness. A red Formica dinette

set with two chairs, a white chipboard cupboard, a tiny fridge, a sink, and a stove. No pictures on the walls, no plants, no photos anywhere in the house. It was a far cry from most of the homey cottage kitchens in the village, and it emphasized that she was an outsider here.

"God—what a night!" she exclaimed, slumping onto a chrome and vinyl chair and taking a big gulp of wine. "And I came here looking for peace and quiet. That's a laugh, isn't it?" She finished the wine with one more slug and put the glass back on the table. "In the first week my kid nearly gets run over and then this." She looked up at him. "There's nowhere really safe, is there?"

"Are you sure you don't have a problem you're not telling me about? Someone you're trying to hide from, maybe?" he asked. "You can tell me, you know. I'm the police. It's my job to protect people."

She shook her head violently. "No. I told you. I'm not running away."

"You must have had a good reason for coming here. It's a long way from Manchester."

She glanced up, and a sad, little smile crossed her lips. "You're going to think it's stupid," she said. "I saw a picture once. My roommate had it on her wall. She came from around here. I thought it was the loveliest place I'd ever seen. There was a blue lake and the mountains and wild flowers and a little white cottage beside the bridge. It was like a fairy-tale scene, like something you see in films. My roommate used to talk about it all the time—how peaceful it was, no crime, no violence. I suppose she was homesick, poor kid, but she made it sound like some sort of paradise." She reached for the bottle and poured herself another glass. "Come on, drink up," she instructed Evan.

"So you came here to get away from crime and violence," he said.

100

"I wanted Jenny to grow up in a decent place, surrounded by decent people," Annie said.

"They're mostly decent people around here," Evan said, "but you can never fully get away from crime and violence, can you? I suppose you weren't at the meeting tonight?"

"I didn't want to leave Jenny. Why, what happened?"

"Two of the men almost came to blows and there was a rare old shouting match."

"All over that ruin the colonel found?"

"Not just that. It was about changing the village name and then about Ted Morgan wanting to build an adventure park here. So you see, we have our own little flare-ups, even in Llanfair."

She nodded again. "Yeah, I've been thinking that this place isn't right for me after all. I'll have a kid who grows up speaking Welsh and I won't be able to talk to her, will I?" She played with the wine glass so that wine slopped over onto the table. "It was another of my stupid dreams. My dad said my crazy ideas would get me in trouble one day. I bet it gives him satisfaction to look down from his cloud and see how right he was."

"So you're not going to stay?"

"I don't think I can. I think now that we'd be better off somewhere else."

"Where?"

"I've no idea."

"Annie, give it a try," Evan said. "Don't go running off again, just because you think someone tried to get into your house. It could be all in your imagination, you know. Or it could have a perfectly reasonable explanation. Maybe some of the local lads playing a prank on a newcomer. I wouldn't put it past them."

"Are you saying that you'd like me to stay?" she asked quietly.

"I'm just saying you should give it a chance," Evan said

101

hastily. He got to his feet. "I must be getting along," he said. "Mrs. Williams will wonder where I've got to and send the police out looking for me."

"I suppose everyone would talk if they found out you'd had a glass of wine with me at this time of night?" Annie said, her cheeky smile returning.

"Talk? We'd never hear the last of it." Evan returned her smile. "In fact, knowing this place, they've probably all heard about it already."

"Sorry if I've ruined your reputation."

She followed him to the front door.

"Most girls would worry about me ruining theirs," Evan commented.

"I don't think I've got much left to ruin," she said.

He opened the door and stepped out into the street. It was raining again, a fine misty rain that collected on eyelashes and hair.

"Thanks for coming, Evan," she said. "I really appreciate everything you've done for me."

"Only—" Evan began, but she cut in. "I know. Only doing your job. You'll never know what a help you've been. It's a pity that—" she broke off. "See yer around," she said and hastily closed the door behind him.

Chapter 11

The next morning Evan had just sat down to breakfast when there was a tap on the back door. Mrs. Williams was halfway from the stove with a plate of fluffy scrambled eggs and crisp bacon in her hands. She must have decided that she had been in mourning for long enough and had started to cook normal meals again. They both looked up, startled by the sudden knocking. Nobody ever came to the back door.

"Now who can that be, and at this hour too?" Mrs. Williams demanded as Evan rose to go to the door.

Outside was a young man in workman's overalls and a cloth cap. Evan had never seen him before.

"They said the local copper lived here." The young man swallowed hard, making his Adam's apple jerk up and down.

"Is something wrong?" Evan asked.

"I think you'd better come and see," the young man said. Evan could see that he was fighting to remain calm.

"But his breakfast is just ready." Mrs. Williams appeared at Evan's shoulder. "You're surely not wanting him to go running off without his breakfast?"

"That's alright. It will stay warm in the oven. I'll be back,"

Evan said. He nodded to the young man. "Alright. Let's go then."

The young man led the way out of the back garden and along the path that ran behind the village. He was walking so fast that Evan almost had to jog to keep up with him.

"He told me to come at eight o'clock this morning, so I turned up like he said," the young man called over his shoulder. "But I couldn't make anyone hear, so I started to look around."

He veered onto the newly graveled drive that led to the four new holiday bungalows and headed toward the first one. When Evan saw where they were going, he realized who the young man must be. This was confirmed by a truck parked a little way down the drive. E. Lloyd, General Contractors, Bangor.

"You're here to work on Ted Morgan's place, are you?"

"That's right." The young man turned back to him again, his face very white.

"Have you tried up at the farm? Maybe he started working without you. He was doing things up there over the weekend."

The young man shook his head violently. "I don't think so," he said. "You'd better come and take a look for yourself, constable, but I think he's been taken ill or something."

He stepped off the path and peered in through the big picture window. The curtains were drawn but there was a narrow gap in the middle. The young man indicated to Evan. "Look in there," he said. "Over behind the sofa. Can you see him?"

In the half darkness of the room the light blue shirt sprawled across the floor was all too visible.

"Yes. I see him," he said. "Did you try the front door?"

"It's locked."

"And he didn't give you a key?"

"No. He told me to meet him here."

"What about a back door?"

"I went round the back," the young man said. "That was locked too."

Evan was examining the front door. "It doesn't look too solid," he said. "Do you reckon we could do it between us?"

"Bust it in, you mean?"

"I don't see any other alternative," Evan said. "We have to get in to him somehow."

"Alright, let's give it a go," the young man said.

The door gave on the third attempt. "We didn't build this place. It must have been Harrisons from Caernarfon—they always buy cheap locks," the young man couldn't resist commenting.

He hung back as Evan stepped inside. "Don't touch anything," Evan called over his shoulder. "I think you'd better wait outside."

"Is he . . . dead?"

Evan looked at the body of Ted Morgan, lying with a surprised expression on his face and an ugly red hole in the middle of his forehead. "Yes," he said quietly. "He's dead. Would you mind standing guard on the place while I go down to the station and call HQ?"

He arrived at the police station door at the same moment as a white van. Sergeant Watkins got out. Evan looked at him in astonishment. "That was quick," he said. "Are you psychic or did someone else call you first?"

"What are you talking about?" Sergeant Watkins said. "I came over because I thought you'd like to know that your hunch was right again. The lab found traces of blood in the soil samples. D.I. Hughes is opening a full investigation. He'll be up here later himself."

"Good, because I've got something else he'll want to see."

"More evidence turned up?"

"No, another body," Evan said. "I was just on my way to call your department. You'd better come up and see for yourself."

"You think this death is suspicious too?" Sergeant Watkins asked, striding out behind Evan as he led the way back to the cottages.

"I'd call it suspicious," Evan said. "He's got a bloody great bullet hole between his eyes."

"Christ," Watkins said. "Don't tell me you've got a serial killer up here."

"It wasn't the same type of killing," Evan said. "But I suppose the deaths have to be linked somehow."

"Someone you knew?"

"Yes. A man called Ted Morgan. He just inherited the farm from his father and came back here to live after twenty years of not setting foot in the place."

The young contractor was still standing guard outside the open front door. Evan could see the relief flood his face at their return.

"Breaking and entering too?" Watkins asked, indicating the broken lock.

"No, that was us," Evan said. "This is the contractor who was supposed to meet Ted Morgan here. He saw the body through the front window and came to get me."

Sergeant Watkins nodded to him. "Stick around, son. We might need to ask you some questions."

He went ahead of Evan into the house. The front door opened directly onto the living room. It was clearly a rental property by the furniture—imitation leather three piece suite, imitation wood table and chairs, small TV and VCR in the corner, bookcase with women's magazines and a few cheap paperbacks, prints of Welsh landscapes on the walls. An efficient room with no character and only a beer bottle on the table to show that it was currently lived in.

"Did you move anything?" Sergeant Watkins asked.

"Nothing was touched at all," Evan said. "As soon as I saw he was dead, I came straight out again."

Watkins looked around the room. "No sign of a struggle,"

he said. He took out his handkerchief and carefully pulled back the curtains. "Ah well, mystery solved," he said with relief in his voice. He bent to indicate Ted Morgan's right hand, half under the sofa. It was clutching a very small pistol. "He shot himself. Suicide."

Evan stared down at Ted Morgan's lifeless face. He looked at the expensive clothes, the gold ring on his finger. He shook his head.

"What?" Sergeant Watkins demanded. "Oh, come on. You're not going to try and tell me it wasn't suicide, are you? He's lying there with the bloody gun in his hand. What more do you want?"

"I can't believe he'd kill himself. That doesn't make sense, sarge. I was with him at a meeting last night. He was looking quite pleased with himself when he told everyone about his grand scheme for this village. And he was due to start remodelling the farmhouse today. Hardly a man about to end it all."

"Maybe he was manic and subject to bouts of depression," Watkins said. "He'd just moved here, you say? What do you know about him?"

"Not much. He seemed like a nice-enough chap. Of course, everyone around here heard all about him when his dad was alive. His father talked about him all the time—how he owned property in London and had made a fortune. Ever so proud of him, Taff was. Pity, because they say he never came home to visit his dad in twenty years."

"And yet he shows up now," Watkins said speculatively. "Money troubles, do you think? The business not doing too well?"

"Hardly," Evan said. "He'd just got planning permission to build a theme park, a big hotel, and a monorail to link them."

"Up here?" Watkins looked surprised.

"He'd bought the old slate quarry. He was going to turn it into an adventure park—The Haunted Mine, he was going to call it."

"Is that a fact?" Watkins shook his head in amazement. "You're right. It doesn't sound like a man who is about to kill himself. And how did the locals like the idea of a theme park in their backyard? I gather they weren't even too thrilled when the Everest Inn was built."

"It's hard to tell," Evan said. "Some of them didn't like the idea, but—" He stopped in midsentence. He remembered all too clearly Evans-the-Meat yelling that he'd kill Ted Morgan to stop him from going ahead with his scheme.

"Didn't like it enough to think of killing him to stop him?" Watkins asked. "That's pretty drastic, isn't it? I wasn't too thrilled when they built that new shopping center behind my house, but I didn't go out and shoot the developers."

Evan nodded. Evans-the-Meat might have been capable of killing Ted Morgan in the heat of the moment, but surely not later in cold blood?

"It could still turn out to be suicide," Watkins said hesitantly. "If he'd found out last night that his financing had collapsed and he wasn't going to be able to go ahead with his project after all? If he was a proud man, maybe he took this way out rather than face the humiliation."

Evan tried to consider what he knew of Ted Morgan. "Of course it will be easy enough to check on his finances," he said. "And as for finding out last night—I haven't noticed a phone in this place."

Watkins sighed. "Alright. I'd better put in a call to the D.I. right away and have him send the medical examiner up here. Maybe we'll know more when he's had a look at the body. In the meantime we should seal off the place."

Evan followed him out of the building. "I'll go and get the tape," he said.

"Do you know who lives in these other new bungalows?" Watkins asked, looking around him with interest.

"They're just holiday homes, let by the week," Evan said. "I'm not sure which of them is occupied right now."

"It might be a good idea to talk to any occupants and see if they heard or saw anything last night. And maybe the people in those houses down below heard something. Sound travels in a valley like this, doesn't it?"

"I'll go and talk to them if you like," Evan said.

"That can wait until we've got the area taped off," Sergeant Watkins said. "You do the taping and I'll put in a call to the D.I. He'll probably forbid us to do anything until he gets here."

The young contractor was standing outside, shifting uncomfortably from one foot to the other. "Is it okay to go yet?" he asked.

"Hang on just a minute longer," Evan said. "I'm coming back to seal off the area. Maybe you could help me."

He accompanied the sergeant down to the police station and left him talking to headquarters while he returned to drape the bushes around the cottage in yellow police tape.

"You reckon he was murdered then?" the young contractor asked, trying to hide the excitement in his voice.

"I don't think it would be wise to speculate at this point," Evan said. "The detective inspector and the medical examiner will be up here soon. Then we'll know more. But thanks for your help. If we can just get you to make a statement, then you're free to go."

"A statement saying what?"

"Anything you think might help us. How Ted Morgan hired you. What he said. What you saw this morning. I'm sorry, it looks like you've been done out of big remodelling job."

The young man nodded, then shrugged. "Oh well, that's life, isn't it? At least I'm still here, which is more than I can say for that poor bloke."

They reached the station together, in time to see Sergeant Watkins putting down the phone. "They're on their way up," he said. "And I bet you can guess the first thing he said to me."

"Have you touched anything?" Evan asked with a grin.

"No. He said, 'Not Evans again? How does he manage to keep turning up bodies?' "

"Look, I came up here for a quiet life," Evan began, then his smile faded. "Funny. That's what Ted Morgan said to me on Sunday." He turned to the young contractor. "You can sit at my desk," he said, "if the sergeant would kindly move out of the chair." He glanced at Sergeant Watkins. "I've asked him to make a statement."

"Quite right." Watkins stood up. "Sit down, son." He watched as Evan handed the man a pen and paper then indicated to Evan that they should go outside. The clouds were rolling back, revealing peaks above, and the sun was starting to break through the mist.

"Going to be a fine day," Evan commented.

Sergeant Watkins looked up at the new holiday bungalows above the village, their windows now winking in the morning sun. "So tell me what you know about Ted Morgan. You say he just got here? Is that why he was living in that place?"

"He owns them," Evan said. "He had them built on the farm property he inherited from his father. That's the old farmhouse up there. He was going to have it completely remodelled. That's why the contractor was here."

"He didn't have any relatives to stay with then?"

"He had a sister and brother-in-law on a farm down the Nantgwnant Pass, but they didn't exactly get along."

"Bad blood in the family, huh?"

"You could put it like that."

"Anyone else you know he didn't get along with?"

Evan sucked in his breath. "Yes," he said at last. "Our local butcher. It seems they've been enemies since childhood." And he went on to recount the entire scene with Evans-the-Meat. "But he'd calmed down by the time we got him home," Evan finished. "He just has a short fuse. He flies into a temper very easily. I'm always separating him from other blokes at the pub."

110

"And you think he'd be capable of killing someone?"

"In a rage maybe," Evan said. "He's a strong man. He might kill someone accidentally and not realize what he was doing. But shooting someone and putting a gun in his hand to make it look like suicide—that doesn't seem the kind of thing he'd do."

"D.I. Hughes will definitely want to talk to him," Watkins said.

"Then we should pop over there first and let him know what's coming," Evan said.

"A good bloke, is he—apart from his homicidal rages?"

Evan smiled. "Yeah, a good bloke. But he's inclined to let his mouth run away with him when he gets upset. I wouldn't want him to say something stupid and get himself into trouble."

"Isn't that called coaching a witness?" Watkins asked. "Okay. Let's wait until the young chap has finished his statement and then we'll visit your mad butcher."

Chapter 12

Evans-the-Meat was just emerging from the walk-in refrigerator carrying a side of lamb as the two policemen came in.

"I'm not open yet," he said, throwing down the carcass on the marble slab and picking up a cleaver. Sergeant Watkins came to an abrupt halt at the sight of the cleaver and the blood-spattered apron. Then the butcher appeared to focus on them and muttered, "Oh, it's you. What do you want?"

"How's the headache this morning, Gareth?" Evan asked.

"I've had worse." Evans-the-Meat started chopping as he spoke.

"This is Detective Sergeant Watkins from Caernarfon, Gareth," Evan said. "He's got some questions he wants to ask you."

"You didn't report me for last night, did you?" Evans-the-Meat demanded. "So I had a couple too many and that fool made me lose my temper—"

"That fool is dead, Gareth," Evan said calmly.

Evans-the-Meat's mouth dropped open. "Ted Morgan is dead?"

"He killed himself last night, apparently," Evan told him.

Evans-the-Meat passed his hand across his face. "Ted Morgan? Killed himself? Go on—you're pulling my leg, aren't you?"

"Deadly serious, sir," Sergeant Watkins said.

Evans-the-Meat laughed uneasily. "I can't say I'm heartbroken by the news. I just find it hard to believe. You didn't know Ted Morgan. He would be the last person on earth to kill himself. He thought too much of himself to do that—always did. Even when he was a little kid he used to carry a comb around in his top pocket and take peeks at himself in all the shop windows. Nah, Ted wasn't a man who'd kill himself on purpose. Was it an accidental overdose, do you think?"

"They found him with a gun in his hand," Evan said.

"Ted Morgan—shoot himself?" Evans-the-Meat shook his head. "Why would he want to do that?"

"That's what we're trying to find out, Mr. Evans," Watkins said. "I hear that you two were old enemies."

Evans-the-Meat passed his tongue nervously over his lips. "Yes, but we hadn't seen each other for twenty-odd years. Besides, why would he want to kill himself just when he was gloating at scoring a triumph over me?"

"My inspector is going to be arriving shortly. I expect he'll want to talk to you, so don't leave town without letting us know, will you?"

"Me? Why would he want to talk to me?" Evans-the-Meat's voice rose. Beads of sweat were visible on his broad forehead. "I had nothing to do with it."

"Just routine, Gareth," Evan said. "Just answer his questions, say no more than you're asked and keep your hair on, okay?"

"What does he think I've got to do with it?" Evans-the-Meat yelled after them, swinging down the meat cleaver with a savage blow that cut the carcass in half.

113

"You're right," Watkins muttered. "He'd make a bad suspect. He had guilt written all over him. But you don't think he did it, do you?"

"If he did, then he's a good actor. All the color drained out of his face when he heard the news. I could swear he was genuinely surprised. And he said he doubted Morgan would ever kill himself. Wouldn't he be anxious to go along with the suicide idea if he was guilty?"

"Then why was he sweating?"

There was no sign of the inspector, but they were just about to go into the police station again when they heard the sound of a car being driven up the pass. Then an ancient black Daimler appeared, slowed, and came to a halt across the street from them. A middle-aged man with shaggy gray hair, faded sweater, and cords got out of it.

"Must be the medical examiner, come on ahead," Sergeant Watkins muttered. "That was quick, wasn't it?"

"Maybe he was out on a case in the area," Evan said.

The man was looking around with a puzzled expression on his face.

"I came here in response from an urgent summons," he said, coming over to them, "but I'm not sure whom the call was from. I've come to look at the remains. Maybe you could direct me."

"I'd be glad to, doctor. We were expecting you," Evan said. "I must say you were pretty sharp about getting here. You've arrived before anyone else."

"Other people are coming to take a look too?" The man looked startled. "I wasn't told."

"Only the usual mob from HQ in Caernarfon," Evan said, "but I don't suppose it will matter if you take a look before they get here."

"I'd appreciate taking a look before anyone else gets here," the man said. "I can't stand people tampering."

114

"I can understand that, sir," Evan said. "It's this way."

"Is it a long walk?" The man looked up at the peaks above. "I'm not sure if I should take foul weather gear."

"It's only just up this little track, sir. A stone's throw away."

"So close? I had no idea. I was given to believe . . ." the man muttered. He followed Evan until they emerged behind the houses bordering the street and the holiday bungalows were visible above.

"There you are, sir," he said. "The one on the far left."

"The one what?" The man couldn't have sounded more surprised.

"The bungalow, sir."

There was a horrified silence, then the man said, "Is this some sort of joke?"

"Oh no, sir. Deadly serious, in fact," Evan said. "There's a body on the floor of the cottage. We need you to take a look at it."

"A mummified body or a skeleton?"

"A fresh body," Evan said. "We found him this morning."

"Why would you want me to take a look at a body?" the man's voice rose to a shriek. "What do you think I could do about it?"

"Establish the time of death," Evan said. He was feeling more and more confused. "You are the police doctor, aren't you?" he demanded.

A look of relief spread across the man's face. "Good lord no, man. I'm the archaeologist from Bangor University. I was asked to come up here and check out a newly discovered site."

Evan started to laugh. After all the tension of last night and then this morning, he laughed helplessly until his whole body shook.

"Are you alright?" Watkins asked with concern.

"I'm sorry." Evan wiped his eye. "But I thought this gen-

tleman was the police doctor come to examine the human remains and he turns out to be the archaeologist come to look at
the remains we discovered on the hill." He turned apologetically to the doctor. "You must have thought I was mad."

"A little eccentric," the man said, smiling now, "but then
I've often found that the inhabitants in these small villages are
a trifle . . . unique." He brushed back his unruly hair from his
forehead. "Now, if you could point out the path to the real remains?"

"Why don't you go to see Mr. Parry Davies? He was the
one who called you. I know he'd love to come up the mountain with you. I would too, but I've got a little matter of a suspicious death we have to take care of."

He pointed the archaeologist in the direction of Chapel
Bethel and went back to join Sergeant Watkins, who was still
waiting impatiently for the arrival of the D.I.

"No sense in hanging around here," Watkins said. "Why
don't we question the occupants of those bungalows and the
people who live down below too. One of them must have
heard a gunshot."

"Alright, sarge," Evan said. "Let's start with the bungalow
next door to Ted's."

The two middle bungalows proved to be unoccupied and
the family in the far end unit was just getting ready to leave
for the beach, loaded up with beach chairs and rubber rings.
No, they hadn't heard or seen anything strange last night, the
woman said impatiently, but then her hubby always dozed in
front of the TV from nine o'clock onwards. She thought she
might have heard a popping noise but she assumed it was a car
backfiring as it came up the pass. And she had no idea what
time it was—any time between nine, when the kids went to
bed, and eleven, when she did. And no, they hadn't seen anything. They drew the curtains when it got dark. They'd never
even seen the occupants of the other cottages.

"That wasn't much help," Watkins commented as they made their way down the hill again. "They must have had that TV blaring away not to have heard a gunshot."

"It was only a little gun, wasn't it?" Evan suggested.

"But that means the occupants of the houses down on the main street aren't likely to have heard anything, unless they sleep with their back windows open."

Evan laughed. "Not too many people sleep with their windows open up here. You'd freeze to death." Then the smile faded as he realized the inappropriateness of this remark with the body lying a few yards away from them. Ted Morgan had been laughing yesterday, full of life . . .

Watkins tapped Evan's arm. "Looks like we'll have to put off the rest of our questioning until later. The big guns have arrived."

A large white police van was coming up the hill. D.I. Hughes was out even before the van was at a complete stop. He looked as Evan remembered him—a dapperly dressed little man with immaculately styled iron-gray hair and a neat line of moustache. Today he was wearing a light blue bow tie with matching silk handkerchief in his top pocket. He'd be nobody's idea of a tough copper, Evan thought, and yet he was annoyingly persistent, like a terrier. He was already looking around like a dog trying to catch a scent as Watkins hurried up to him.

"Where's the body then?" he demanded.

"Up in one of those holiday bungalows," Watkins said.

"A tourist then?"

"No, a local, but only recently come back here. He owned them and he was living in one while he had the farmhouse remodelled."

"Who found the body?" Hughes asked, walking so fast that Watkins had trouble keeping up with him.

"A local contractor who'd come to work on the farmhouse, sir."

"Is the contractor still here?"

"We let him go, but we got a complete statement and his phone number."

"Good man."

Evan hung back by the van, not sure if his presence was required or even welcome. The D.I. had made it very clear on his last murder case that he wanted no interference from village policemen.

The police medical officer had now emerged from the van with his black bag, and a couple of forensic technicians were getting their stuff out of the back.

"Up there, is it?" the doctor asked Evan pleasantly.

"Yes, sir. The one on the left," Evan answered.

"Why is that bodies always seem to involve an uphill walk in Wales?" the doctor wondered. "Were you the first officer on the scene?"

Evan fell into step beside him, glad that he now had an excuse to accompany them back to the crime scene.

"The contractor saw something suspicious through the window and came to get me just before eight o'clock," Evan said. "I saw what looked like a body lying on the floor so we broke the door down between us."

"Did you move him at all?"

"Didn't need to, sir," Evan said. "He was obviously dead. There was a nasty hole in the middle of his forehead."

"Any sign of the weapon?"

"The gun is still in his hand, sir."

"Ah. A suicide then."

"Not necessarily," Evan said cautiously. He didn't want to be told to leave the detecting to detectives.

The doctor looked up sharply.

"He was a man who had just announced big plans to the whole village. And the general opinion is that he thought a lot of himself. It just doesn't make sense that he'd kill himself now."

"Some people are good at hiding the turmoil inside," the doctor said. "But we'll be able to tell soon enough whether he shot himself, I'd imagine."

He passed ahead of Evan into the small living room. D.I. Hughes was examining the hand with the gun in it. "It seems a clear enough case of suicide to me, doctor," he said in his crisp voice. "We'll need to establish time of death and that's about it."

"We might as well get pictures and have the lab boys go over the room, just in case anything irregular turns up later," the police doctor said, glancing back at Evan.

D.I. Hughes gaze focussed on Evan too. "Don't tell me that the constable here has been coming up with more wild theories," he said with an exasperated sigh. "Amateur detectives in the force are the last thing we need."

"All the same sir," Watkins ventured, "it does seem strange that he chose last night to kill himself. Apparently he'd just shown the whole village his plans to build a new resort here, and he'd just started to remodel the farmhouse. Why bother if you were planning to kill yourself?"

"Ask Dawson to take some photos of his hand, will you, Watkins," the inspector said after a pause. "Let's see if we can tell whether his finger pulled the trigger. Get the lab boys to test for gunpowder residue, and then let's see what prints show up on the gun."

"Would you like me to question the neighbors, sir, and see if any of them actually heard the shot?" Evan asked cautiously.

"You could do that, I suppose," the D.I. said with no great enthusiasm. "Why don't you go with him, Watkins?"

"It's pretty obvious that he doesn't think he can trust me to do anything without messing it up," Evan commented to the sergeant as they walked down the hill together.

"It's more likely he doesn't want you to pull another scoop on us. He took a lot of ragging about that after those murders

119

on the mountain. He didn't take kindly to being outmanoeuvered by a local P.C."

"It was only luck that I stumbled on the killer first," Evan said.

"Of course it wasn't. You were on the right track all along," Watkins said. "And the more I think of it, the more I get the feeling that you're right about this not being a suicide. Why go to the trouble of getting planning permission and hiring contractors if you're going to kill yourself? And there was no note either. People who shoot themselves usually leave notes justifying the deed, don't they?"

"And he just didn't look like a man about to kill himself," Evan said. "I spoke to him the day before and he seemed relaxed, enjoying life."

Watkins nodded. "Which means we'd be dealing with two murders then. You reckon the same person is responsible for both? They weren't the same type of crime, were they?"

"I don't want to think that we might have two killers in the neighborhood," Evan said, "and the two murders did have something in common."

"Like what?"

"They were both sneaky crimes, weren't they? The first death was made to look like an accident. The second one is made to look like a suicide. These are the acts of a person who thinks on his feet."

"Or her feet," Watkins added. "So you say Morgan didn't get along with his sister and brother-in-law, and we know he didn't get along with Evans the butcher. Anyone else who might have wanted him out of the way?"

"Not that I know of," Evan said. "But then he'd just got here. I know nothing of his life in London. Someone could have followed him here."

"The same person who also had a grudge against the colonel?" Watkins asked.

Evan stared out down the pass, thinking. "I find that hard

to believe," he said. "I'd say that Ted Morgan and the colonel would have moved in totally different circles. A young flashy businessman and a stodgy old retired colonel living on a pension? Who could have a bone to pick with both of them?"

"They did have something in common," Watkins suggested. "They both came from London and they both just got here."

"That's true, but I imagine there are five hundred holidaymakers from London in the area at this moment."

"You're the one who's hot on connections," Watkins said. "Think up some."

They had reached the row of cottages on the main street. Evan knocked on the first door. As they went down the row they got the same answer over and over again. Nobody had heard a gunshot, but that wasn't too surprising. An Arnold Schwarzenegger movie was on TV starting at nine-thirty, full of explosions and gunfire. A TV pollster would have been delighted by the hundred percent viewing of one channel.

Nobody had seen or heard anything out of the ordinary, that is until they came to young Mrs. Rees.

"I did see one thing," she said, staring out of the window as if to confirm what she had seen. "I was upstairs in the front bedroom. Our Glynis had a fever and I was just bringing her a drink of water when I happened to look out of the window. I saw someone come out of the path between this row of houses and the police station and hurry across the street. Then I saw a front door open."

"Could you see who it was?"

"I couldn't see the person but I think I could tell which front door it was," Mrs. Rees said. "It was this end of the row of shops. It must have been Evans-the-Meat."

"Evans-the-Meat? You mean when we brought him home after the meeting—around nine o'clock?"

"No. Later than that. Everyone had already gone home. The street was deserted and he was all alone."

"What now?" Evans-the-Meat demanded belligerently as the two policemen came back into his shop. "All these coppers hanging around is bad for trade, you know."

"I thought I told you to stay home last night, Gareth Evans," Evan said. "I told you to go straight to bed."

"And I did!"

"You were seen crossing the street, coming from the direction of Ted Morgan's bungalow," Evan said.

"I was never—" Evans-the-Meat began.

Sergeant Watkins stepped forward. "Mr. Evans, it doesn't look good for you right now. I must warn you that you have the right to remain silent, but anything you say may be taken down and used as evidence against you."

Evans-the-Meat turned terrified eyes to Evan. "You've got to help me, Evan bach," he said. "I didn't kill anybody. I swear it."

"You threatened to, Gareth. The whole town heard you."

"You know what I'm like when my temper is up. I say things I don't really mean."

"And do things you don't really mean?" Watkins asked.

"Constable Evans knows I cool down again quickly enough," Evans-the-Meat said. "I'd cooled down by the time I got home."

"But you went to Ted Morgan's place, didn't you?" Evan demanded. "Why else would you be crossing the street? The path only leads to those bungalows."

"Alright, so I went there," Evans-the-Meat confessed. "The more I thought about it, the more I knew I had to have it out with him. I wanted to try and talk sense into that jackass, to make him see that he'd ruin Llanfair for all of us if he went ahead with his bloody stupid scheme."

"So you went to his bungalow. What time was this?" Sergeant Watkins asked.

Evans-the-Meat shook his head. "It couldn't have been later than nine-thirty, quarter to ten."

"And what did you say to him?"

"I didn't go in," Evans-the-Meat said. "When I got there I saw that he had someone with him. The curtains were drawn and I could see two shapes moving around. I could hear Ted talking to someone—talking and laughing, he was. So I just turned around and went back home."

"Could you tell who was with him, sir?" Watkins asked.

"No idea. Like I said, the curtains were drawn and there wasn't much light in the room. I just saw shadows and Ted was doing all the talking as usual."

"Did you happen to hear what he was saying?"

"Something about being old friends and picking up where they left off." Evans-the-Meat shrugged. "That could apply to half the village. We were all in school together, weren't we?"

"How long did you hang around up there?"

"No time at all. I knew I'd feel stupid if someone came out and saw me standing there, so I went back home again." He grabbed Evan's sleeve. "You've got to believe me. I didn't kill him!"

Chapter 13

The news of Ted Morgan's death had already spread throughout the village. Upstairs windows and front doors were open as housewives excitedly passed on the information.

Evans-the-Milk pulled up his van beside Evan and Watkins. "Then it's true what they're saying, is it? Ted Morgan shot himself last night? Who would have thought it? You could have knocked me down with a feather when Mrs. Hopkins told me. That's what comes of living in London, isn't it? All that fast living and those unhealthy fumes." He drove on again to spread the word up the rest of the village street.

"There's no chance of hiding anything in a place like this, is there?" Watkins muttered to Evan as they crossed the street.

"The bush telegraph is amazing here," Evan said. "By now it will probably be all round the village by now that we've been to talk to Evans-the-Meat. Let's hope nobody spills the beans to the D.I. before we get back to him."

"And you'd better hope that the M.O. brings in a verdict of suicide, or things don't look good for your pal Evans-the-Meat."

Evan glanced back at the butcher's shop. He could see the burly butcher still standing motionless, staring at them.

"He had an explanation," Evan ventured.

"Which no jury is going to believe, you know that. And he had the motive. And witnesses to his threats."

"I know," Evan agreed. "You're right. Things don't look good for him. Do we have to mention this to the D.I. yet?"

"Why shouldn't we?"

"Because I don't think he did it."

"He wanted the man dead, for Pete's sake. He tried to kill him in front of a couple of hundred witnesses. He admits he went to the house and we've only got his word that he didn't go in. What was there to stop him from carrying out his threats? What more do you want?"

"Nothing, except . . ." Evan began hesitantly.

"Except what?"

"It wasn't his kind of crime. If Ted Morgan had been strangled or cut in half with the meat cleaver, then Evans-the-Meat would be my prime suspect, but only when he was drunk and angry enough. But a neat little bullet between the eyes—that's not like him at all."

"That little gun would have been easy to hide in a pocket, in case he bumped into you again."

Evan laughed uneasily. "I can't believe Evans-the-Meat owns a gun like that. A bloody great hunting rifle, maybe, but not that little thing."

"You could be right," Watkins said. "Let's hear what brilliant deductions the D.I. has come up with first. He might have the case solved by now." He gave Evan a wink as he pushed open the door that led to the police station.

The grandly named community police substation, Llanfair and district, was actually only one room, with a large closet and lavatory at one end. D.I. Hughes was on the phone to HQ and motioned them to be quiet as they came in.

125

"I should be able to let you know shortly when we're releasing the body," he said into the phone. "Oh, and Mavis, brew a pot of coffee for me, would you? I'll be back soon. Thanks, Mavis, you're a sweetie pie." He put down the phone in time to catch Watkins and Evan exchanging a look. "The doctor should be down here in a minute," he said. "He puts the time of death at no later than ten P.M."

"That's interesting," Evan blurted out.

"In what way?" the D.I. asked coldly.

"I only meant that I must have just missed seeing the killer—if there was a killer," Evan explained hastily. "I was out on the street myself, making sure that there was no more trouble after the meeting." He regretted saying the words as soon as they were out of his mouth.

"Trouble? What kind of trouble?"

"There was a village meeting," Evan said. "It got a little heated, as these things sometimes do." He looked across at Watkins, willing him not to mention that Evans-the-Meat had tried to kill Ted Morgan and had to be dragged away.

"Morgan was at the meeting?" D.I. Hughes asked sharply.

"Yes, sir, the whole village was," Evan said, again before Watkins could say anything. He had a feeling that the D.I. would pounce on Evans-the-Meat as a suspect the moment he heard the details, and then not bother to look for anyone else.

"So what time did this meeting finish?" Hughes asked.

"It broke up around nine. I stayed out in the street, making sure everyone got home, until about nine fifteen. Then I was called out again about nine-thirty."

"Called out—to what?" D.I. Hughes asked, looking up from the doodles he was making around his notes.

"Oh, a woman thought someone was trying to break into her house. It turned out to be a false alarm." Evan felt himself flushing.

126

"And you didn't see anything suspicious while you were out?"

"No, sir. The whole place was deserted."

"Which, of course, goes along with the idea of suicide," the inspector said, going back to his doodles. He was drawing neat boxes within boxes around each word. It figured, Evan thought.

The door opened and the medical examiner came in. He pulled up a chair and sat down opposite the detective inspector.

"Seen all you need to up there?" D.I. Hughes asked.

The doctor nodded. "I've done all I can for the moment. I suggest we let the Home Office pathologist take a look for confirmation, but I can tell you right now that it wasn't suicide."

"It wasn't suicide?" D.I. Hughes' face was a mask of stone. He hated being wrong. He hated it doubly in the presence of subordinates, especially village bobbies. "How can you be so sure?"

The doctor grinned. "He'd have needed bloody long arms. He was shot from at least five feet away. Oh, and one of your men working up there says to tell you there were two sets of prints on the gun—Morgan's and one other, but they were both smudged as if someone had tried to wipe it clean at some stage."

"Any other significant prints in the room?" the D.I. asked.

"Plenty. It was let to different people every week, wasn't it? And I don't suppose they washed the walls in between."

The D.I. frowned and started doodling again. "That puts a whole different complexion on things," he said. "You're sure about the five feet?"

"Based on the entry and the amount of damage the bullet did. I've seen enough people who have shot themselves at close range. It's usually messier."

"Damn," the D.I. said. "Alright, let's start at square one.

Is there anyone you can think of who might have wanted to kill Ted Morgan?"

"A couple of people we know didn't get along with him," Evan said, "but he just moved here from London. It could have been a complete outsider."

"Let's work on the ones we know about first," the D.I. said. "Who were they?"

Before Evan could answer the door was flung open again, sending a great gust of air through the room. The D.I. slapped his hand to hold the papers on the desk as a young woman came in. It was hard to say who looked more surprised—the policemen or Annie Pigeon.

"Oh," she said, stopping short. "I didn't realize you had company."

"Did you need something, Annie, because we're very busy at the moment," Evan said. "The inspector and his sergeant have come up from Caernarfon."

"I heard," Annie said. "It's all over the village, isn't it? Imagine. That poor man, only just got here like me. It gave me the shivers all over."

"Do you have something that we can help you with, Ms. . . . ?" D.I. Hughes interrupted impatiently.

"Pigeon. Annie Pigeon. I came down to file my report," Annie said.

"Report?" the D.I. asked.

"On the break-in last night. The constable told me to come down here in the morning so we could write the official report."

"Ah, so you were the person who called out Constable Evans last night?" Evan could see the D.I. giving Annie the once-over. She was wearing jeans that fitted her like a second skin and a low necked T shirt with Bugs Bunny on it. Better than the halter top and tiny shorts, but not much.

"I thought someone was trying to get into my house again," she said, going up to the desk and leaning down confidentially toward the D.I. "I heard him at the back door. I was that scared I had to call in Constable Evans."

"But Constable Evans didn't manage to find anybody?"

Evan shook his head. "I searched all over. It could have been the wind. It makes strange noises up here and there are bushes behind her house."

"You said again?" Sergeant Watkins asked, suddenly alert from his chair in the corner. "Are you saying that someone tried to break in before?"

"On Sunday," Annie said, turning to him. "I was out for a little walk with Constable Evans and when I got back the kitchen window was open. I looked around, but I couldn't see that anything had been taken, so I thought I might have been imagining things. It's the first time I've lived alone, you know, and in a strange place too, so maybe I'm a bit jumpy."

"Ah, so you think now that you only imagined it on both occasions?" D.I. Hughes asked, tapping his pencil impatiently. He clearly wanted Annie out of there so that they could get back to business.

"That's what I decided," Annie said. "I told myself I was being daft and it was all in my head." She paused dramatically. "Until I heard about the shooting this morning. Then I remembered the gun. I don't know why I didn't think of it before. I ran up to look for it and it was gone."

D.I. Hughes was no longer tapping his pencil or doodling. He leaned forward, staring at her. "Are you saying that you owned a gun and that gun is now missing?"

"Yes, sir," Annie said. "That's why I hurried down here to see Constable Evans."

"Why exactly did you own a gun, Miss Pigeon?" Sergeant Watkins asked. "You have a permit for it, I hope."

"Oh yeah, it's all legal," Annie said. "I lived in a bad part of London once. A friend bought me the gun just in case, after a girl was raped on my street. I've never had to use it, thank God, but I hung onto it. I kept it at the back of my undies

129

drawer, actually. I'd forgotten all about it until this." She looked around the room excitedly. "You don't mean to tell me that the murder was done with my gun?"

The D.I. leaned forward in his seat. "Could you describe it for us, Miss Pigeon?"

"It didn't really look like a real gun at all. It was a pretty little thing, with a pearl handle. I remember saying that I didn't believe a little thing like that could ever kill anybody . . ." She caught the expression on Sargeant Watkins' face. "Was that it? Then someone did break in on Sunday. I must go through all my stuff again. I wonder what else he could have taken."

"Can you tell us about your own movements yesterday evening, Miss Pigeon?" D.I. Hughes asked.

"My movements?" Annie looked shocked. "I didn't go out all evening."

"Not even to the village meeting?"

"Why would I go to that? I just moved here and I don't speak Welsh. Besides, I've got a little girl. I couldn't leave her home alone, could I?"

"So you stayed home all evening?"

"Here, what are you getting at?" Annie demanded. "You're not suggesting I might have had something to do with killing that bloke, are you? I didn't know him from Adam. I only met him the day before. I don't go around killing complete strangers, you know." She looked from one face to the next. "Do you know what time he was killed?"

"Before ten o'clock, the doctor here says," Sergeant Watkins said.

A big smile spread across Annie's face. "There you are then. Constable Evans can vouch for me. He came to my house around nine-thirty and he didn't leave until ten-fifteen at the earliest."

Evan felt all the eyes in the room turn to him. "I told you sir. She called to report a suspected break-in."

130

"And it took you forty-five minutes to decide that nobody was there?" Evan could detect sarcasm in the D.I.'s voice.

"Oh no," Annie chimed in before Evan could speak. "He helped me get Jenny to sleep and then we had a glass of wine together. I needed to steady my nerves. Constable Evans was a big comfort to me."

"I'm sure he was," the inspector said. He exchanged a dry look with the medical examiner. Evan wanted to tell him that it wasn't the way it sounded. "So you and Miss Pigeon were together from nine-thirty until ten-fifteen, constable?"

"Yes, sir," Evan said, feeling his face glowing with embarrassment. "She was rather upset, sir," he added.

D.I. Hughes got to his feet. "Well, thank you for coming forward so promptly, Miss Pigeon. You've saved us a lot of time and effort and we appreciate it. Now, if you wouldn't mind letting Constable Evans take a set of fingerprints before you go."

"Fingerprints? My fingerprints? What for?" Annie shot Evan an alarmed look. "I told you, I was home all evening. And someone broke in and took my gun. That's the fingerprints you want to be looking for, I'd say."

D.I. Hughes put a neatly manicured hand on Annie's shoulder. "There's no cause for alarm, I assure you, Miss Pigeon. It makes good sense to have your fingerprints on file. They'd be on the gun, wouldn't they, if it belonged to you?"

"I suppose so," Annie said hesitantly, "but I told you, I haven't touched it in years. It was wrapped up in an old nightie, so all the fingerprints might have been rubbed off by now."

"We usually manage to find one or two," Sergeant Watkins said. "And we'll need to know which are yours so that we can see who else might have handled it."

"Oh, I see. Yes." Annie visibly relaxed. She held out her hands to Evan. "You'll mind my nail polish, won't you? I just did it yesterday."

131

"I won't spoil your nails," Evan said, opening the ink pad and taking her hand. "And I think Miss Pigeon has a point, sir," he said, turning to the inspector. "It would be a good idea to look for prints around her window frame and back door. It's possible that the same person who took her gun also committed the murder."

"The interesting thing to me is how anybody knew she owned a gun," the inspector said. "Did you tell anybody about this gun, Miss Pigeon?"

"Not here," Annie said. "I don't really know anybody here yet. Of course my friends back home knew."

"Is it possible that somebody followed you here, with the intention of getting hold of your gun?" Sergeant Watkins asked. "Is there anyone you can think of who might do that?"

Annie shook her head violently. "No one. No one at all."

"You say you've just moved here, Miss Pigeon?" D.I. Hughes asked. "Why did you chose Llanfair? Do you have a job here?"

"No sir. I'm home taking care of my three year old," Annie said. "I came here because I wanted her to grow up away from crime and violence." She gave a short, bitter laugh. "That's bloody funny, isn't it? Been here two weeks and we've had two murders."

"Two?" The D.I. looked confused. "Oh yes, the colonel. Yes, it does look as if his death wasn't accidental after all. Well, I'm sorry you've had such an unfortunate start to your stay in Llanfair, Miss Pigeon. I assure you that this kind of thing isn't normal for our little corner of Wales."

Annie gave a twisted smile as she took the paper towel Evan was offering her and started wiping her fingers. "Maybe I'm the jinx," she said. "Who knows, maybe I bring bad luck wherever I go." She looked around the room. "Am I free to leave now?"

"Yes, thank you. We have all that we need, I think." D.I. Hughes looked to Sergeant Watkins for confirmation. "But please don't leave the area without notifying us first," he added as Annie reached the door.

Annie looked back nervously. "I'm not allowed to go any-where? Why not?"

"We will need you to identify the gun officially at an in-quest," Sergeant Watkins said.

"I wasn't planning on going any further than the beach anyway," Annie said. "I don't have the money to travel right now. Ta-ta for now then. See yer around, Evan."

And she was gone.

"Interesting," D.I. Hughes said as the door closed behind her. "She comes here and someone tries to break into her house and takes her gun. I think that young woman has a few things she's not telling us. Just how well do you know her, Constable Evans?" It was more accusation than question.

Evan felt himself flushing again and cursed his fair Celtic skin. "Only what you've heard about, sir. I met her last week. She asked me to show her the area on Sunday and she called me in about the break-in last night."

"And you think this break-in was genuine?"

Evan shrugged. "I'd say she was genuinely scared, sir. Her hand was shaking so much she could hardly pick up her wine glass and then she knocked it back in one gulp."

"We may be dealing with an alcohol problem there," the inspector said.

"I haven't noticed any alcohol before, sir," Evan said. "And she didn't smell of booze when I first arrived."

"But you definitely found no signs of a break-in?"

"None at all, sir."

"She claims it was the second attempt, doesn't she, sir," Watkins suggested. "If someone broke in on Sunday and took the gun then, why come back the next night?"

"And why did she only discover the gun was missing this morning?" D.I. Hughes retorted. "That would be the first thing you'd check on, wouldn't it?"

"Not if she hadn't ever used it, sir," Evan said. "Maybe she just hung onto it from habit."

"Well, you've given her a cast-iron alibi for last night, constable," the inspector said, "but I wonder if she's not mixed up in this somehow. There has to be an unsavory boyfriend lurking in the background, someone who knew she had a gun."

"Someone she's too frightened of to admit he's terrorizing her?" Sergeant Watkins added. "She had to be running away from someone to suddenly show up here out of nowhere, didn't she?"

The D.I. nodded. "Run a background check on her, Watkins, and let's see what we come up with. And, Evans, stay friendly for now. She's obviously got her eye on you. Encourage her. Maybe she'll get comfortable enough to confide in you."

Evan tried not to wince. It was easy enough for the D.I. to suggest encouraging Annie Pigeon. But the D.I. didn't have Bronwen watching his every move. How could he ever make her understand that this was all in the line of duty?

Evan had to admit that he felt sorry for Annie Pigeon and he wanted to help her. He suspected, like the D.I., that she was keeping things back from him. Maybe his presence would protect her from an abusive boyfriend. Maybe she was in danger right now if the boyfriend was somehow involved in the killing of Ted Morgan. Because Annie Pigeon clearly knew more than she was telling. She'd shown that just now. She had called the colonel's death a murder when Evan had been very careful to let the village think that it was still an accident.

Chapter 14

"I think we need to do a little brainstorming before we go any further," D.I. Hughes said, motioning to Evan to join them at the table. "Miss Pigeon brought up an important point. She reminded me that we are dealing with two murders in this village, not one."

Evan decided that the D.I. didn't miss much.

"We need to decide how these two deaths could possibly be connected. Let's hear your opinion, sergeant."

"Well, sir," Sergeant Watkins began, "at first glance I can't see how they could be connected. They're not the same kind of crimes, are they? One is a crime of violence. It took a strong, violent person to bash in someone's skull and then throw him in the river. But anyone could have committed the second crime, even a slightly built woman. All it needed was good aim and catching Ted Morgan by surprise. And it was a woman's weapon, don't forget."

"So what do the two deaths have in common, constable?"

Evan cleared his throat. He felt as if he was back in school, facing a difficult master. "The only links I can see, are that both the victims arrived here recently and they both came from London."

"Important points!" the D.I. said. "Make a note of that, will you, Watkins."

"But they would hardly have moved in the same circles in London, sir," Evan went on. "Ted Morgan was a successful businessman. The colonel was living on a small pension and he only went to his old army club. And London's a big place."

"And Miss Pigeon—did she come from London too?"

"No, sir. She said she came from Manchester."

"Manchester? She doesn't speak like a Lancashire lass, does she?"

"She might just have meant that she was living there before she came here," Evan said.

"Possibly. But there is a link in that she has also just arrived. Make a note of that too, sergeant."

Sergeant Watkins frowned as he scribbled on his pad.

"Of course, our first line of enquiry should be the most direct." D.I. Hughes went on, looking around the table as if he was really enjoying himself now. "What's the first question we detectives are trained to ask ourselves? Who benefits financially from the death? And who does here?"

"The next of kin would be Ted Morgan's sister," Evan said. "She's married and lives just down the mountain near Beddgelert."

"Then I suggest that Sergeant Watkins goes to talk to this sister before we do anything more," D.I. Hughes said. "I want to get back to the crime scene. There are always little clues that the lab boys overlook." He reached into his pocket and took out a magnifying glass. "If you'd like to accompany me back up there, doctor?"

"Exit Holmes and Watson," Sergeant Watkins muttered to Evan as the two men went out. "Did you notice the magnifying glass? He really uses that thing. Oh well, if it keeps him happy and out of our hair." He got to his feet. "Ready to go pay a visit on Morgan's sister then?"

"You want me to come along?" Evan asked, pleased but apprehensive. "You don't think the D.I. will mind?"

"I have to take you along with me," Watkins said. "You know my Welsh isn't that great. I need an interpreter." He grinned at Evan as he headed for the door.

Sam and Gwyneth Hoskins were just sitting down to their midday meal when Evan and Sergeant Watkins knocked on their cottage door. Gwyneth showed them into a dark, low-ceilinged kitchen where Sam was in the middle of carving thick, pink slices from a leg of lamb.

"So it's true then, is it?" Gwyneth asked, wiping her hands nervously on her apron.

"You've already heard the news then?" Evan asked.

Gwyneth's eyes darted from Evan to Sergeant Watkins. "Elspeth Rees called me this morning. I couldn't rightly believe it. Our Ted, taking his own life?" She shook her head firmly. "There's never been any insanity in the family."

Sam Hoskins had finished with the meat and was now spooning heaps of pickled cabbage onto the plate beside it. "Excuse me for eating," he muttered, "but I've got to get back to the sheep. Farmers don't have the luxury of lunch breaks, do they?"

"He only came in this minute just," Gwyneth said, glancing across at Sam. "I wasn't rightly sure what to do. I thought Sam would never believe it. Not our Ted. He wasn't the type, was he?"

"You're right. He might not have been the type, Mrs. Hoskins," Sergeant Watkins said dryly. "It appears now that someone else might have pulled the trigger and made it look like suicide."

"That's more like it," Sam Hoskins said with a mouthful of lamb and bread. "I'd imagine there were plenty of folk who'd be quite happy to take a potshot at our Ted."

"Hush now, Sam. Don't go talking like that," Gwyneth whispered in a shocked voice. "You shouldn't talk ill of the dead."

"He got what he deserved," Sam said, cutting himself another huge mouthful of lamb and shoving it into his mouth.

Gwyneth looked appealingly at the policemen. "I won't say there was any love lost between Ted and me," she said. "I can't say that I'd weep for him now. He always was the baby, the darling who could do no wrong. But he was a sadistic little bugger—I remember he killed my pet rabbit then had the nerve to pretend to our dad that he'd been out hunting and shot a rabbit, and he got the credit for it too. I more or less raised him after our ma died. He was six and I was ten, but he never showed an ounce of gratitude when he grew up. He couldn't wait to get out here and never came back until now."

"And never sent as much as a Christmas card to us, did he, Gwyneth love?" Sam Hoskins asked as he picked up a mug of tea.

"So you can think of people who would have liked to take a potshot at Ted Morgan, can you, Mr. Hoskins?" Evan asked quietly, "Beside yourself, I mean?"

"What are you saying, Mr. Evans?" Gwyneth demanded. "You're not saying my Sam might have had something to do with it, are you?"

"Not at all, Mrs. Hoskins. I was wondering if you or your husband could come up with the names of some people who didn't like Ted Morgan, enough to kill him."

"Plenty, I should think," Sam Hoskins said. "He always enjoyed baiting people and getting into fights with them. Evans-the-Meat for one. Those two were always scrapping when they were little. And I hear that Evans-the-Meat went for him at the village meeting last night."

"You weren't there yourself?" Evan asked.

138

"Why would we be there? What they do in the village of Llanfair doesn't concern us," Gwyneth said quickly. "Besides, we don't like to stay up late."

"So do you mind telling us where you were last night from about eight o'clock onwards?"

"That's a bloody stupid question," Sam Hoskins spluttered. "We're up at four in the morning, this time of year. We go to bed around nine, don't we?"

"So you were home, in bed?" Sergeant Watkins said. "I don't suppose you can prove that."

"I don't keep a harem in the bedroom closet who could vouch for me, unfortunately. Just the one wife."

Evan had to smile.

"We haven't found his will yet, but it's possible that you're his primary beneficiary, Mrs. Hoskins," Sergeant Watkins said.

"You mean I inherit his money?" Gwyneth asked, her face lighting up.

"And the farm, I shouldn't wonder," Sam added.

"Fancy that." Gwyneth's cheeks were very pink as she glanced at Sam. "I can't take it in yet. It's all too sudden." She put her hand to her heart and stood there shaking her head. "When do you think I'll know?"

"You'll probably hear from his solicitor's office when they've sorted out the will," Sergeant Watkins said. "And when they've found your brother's killer. By the way, Mr. Hoskins, do either of you own a gun?"

"Of course I've got a gun," Sam Hoskins said. "And I use it if I see a fox anywhere near my lambs." He opened a corner cupboard and took out an ancient shotgun.

"Thanks, that's all for now then," Sergeant Watkins said. "Sorry to disturb your lunch."

"Not at all. Especially when you're bringing what's good news for us, right?" Sam Hoskins said, jabbing his fork in a pickled onion.

Gwyneth showed the policemen to the front door, closed it behind her, and came back to the table. "All the same, Sam," she said quietly, "I think you should have told them where you were last night. They're going to find out anyway and then it looks bad for us, doesn't it?"

"They won't find out a thing if you don't blab, woman," Sam Hoskins said and calmly went on eating.

"So what did you think?" Watkins asked Evan as they drove up the hill again. "Any possibility he could have done it?"

"Possible, but not probable," Evan said. "Can you see him using that dainty little pistol? He showed you what he uses—a bloody great shotgun. I can see him bashing Ted over the head, the way the colonel was bashed, but not shooting him like that. For one thing, Ted would be on his guard with Sam. His expression showed that he was completely taken by surprise."

Watkins nodded. "What about her then?"

"Gwyneth? I wouldn't have thought she had the nerve. She comes across to me as a timid little thing."

"But not as innocent as she wants us to think," Watkins said. "She had clearly thought about the money aspect before we got there. Her surprise and delight were too phony. And it's likely she's going to be quite a rich woman."

"But why choose that particular evening when everyone was out and about for the meeting?" Evan asked. "Most nights you could walk up the village street at ten and not see a soul."

"You've got a point there," Watkins said. "So it had to be someone who wanted to make sure Ted didn't go through with his grand scheme for the adventure park—which points to Evans-the-Meat again, I'm afraid. We'll have to let the D.I. know about him."

140

Evan nodded. "We don't really have a choice, even though I'm pretty sure he didn't do it."

"Well done, lads." Detective Inspector Hughes slapped his hand on the desk with a rare display of enthusiasm. "I think we've hit a hole in one. I knew there would be an easy answer to this. Now all we need to do is find just one fingerprint or one little clod of mud and we've got him. The lab boys are almost done up there, and I've made good and sure they've got everything for analysis."

"I bet you have, sir," Watkins said dryly. Evan stopped himself from smiling.

"So what about a spot of lunch?" D.I. Hughes suggested. "Do they do a decent meal at your local pub, Evans?"

"If you like meat pies and sausage rolls," Evan said.

The D.I. shuddered.

"They don't have much lunchtime trade," Evan added apologetically, "Harry-the-Pub can't cook. Neither can Betsy."

"Then we better get on down to Caernarfon. They do a decent fettuccine at the Prince of Wales." The D.I. was still looking pleased with himself. "I think it might be a good idea to take our belligerent butcher down with us for questioning. That usually puts the fear of God in them, doesn't it? Go and bring him in, Watkins."

"Bring him here, sir? Now?" Watkins asked with a glance at Evan.

"Of course. I want to get this case squared away." D.I. Hughes snapped. "What are you waiting for?"

"Sir, I really don't think he's your man," Evan said cautiously. "I know it looks bad for him, but—"

"Nonsense, constable. What more do you want? He tries to kill Ted Morgan in full view of a whole room full of people. He has to be dragged home, drunk. He admits sneaking out to go to Morgan's house later. He had the motive. He had the opportunity." He looked up at Watkins and Evan with a satisfied smile. "There may be promotions in this, who knows. Go on then, bring him here."

"You'd better come along, Evans," Watkins said. "And bring the handcuffs. He might not come quietly."

"I don't think for a moment that he will come quietly," Evan said as they left the D.I. in the station. "I'd probably put up a struggle if I was being arrested for something I didn't do."

Watkins moved closer to Evan. "Don't go overboard with this loyalty thing, will you? You know what the D.I.'s like when he's onto a hunch. The only way to make him change his mind is to find someone who had a better reason to kill Morgan. And you could be wrong, you know."

"You mean Evans-the-Meat might have done it?" Evan asked. He shook his head. "Killed Ted maybe, but he'd never have bashed the poor old colonel over the head. He thought a lot of the colonel and he was so excited that the colonel had found the ruin, too."

But somebody wasn't, Evan thought, as they waited to cross the street. It was possible that somebody hadn't wanted that call put through to the archaeologists in the morning— someone who wanted to stop any kind of development or publicity at all in Llanfair, be it a famous ruin or a new hotel complex. Was there anybody who fitted that description?

"Oh no, not again!" Evans-the-Meat looked up with a resigned scowl as the two policemen came back into his shop. "What is it this time?"

"The D.I. wants to talk to you," Watkins said. "Over at the police station."

"Let him come and talk to me here. I'm busy," Evans-the-Meat growled.

"You're wanted at the station, Evans," Watkins said. "Now."

Evans-the-Meat's face flushed scarlet. "Who do you think

you are, ordering people around. It's not the bloody gestapo here, you know."

"You're wanted for questioning, Evans," Watkins said, "and we need your fingerprints. So get moving."

"But I told you what happened last night," Evans-the-Meat said, his voice rising. "I told you I went to Ted's house but I didn't go in."

"And now you can tell that to the D.I.," Watkins said.

Evans-the-Meat's hand gripped at his meat cleaver. "Look, I've told you I had nothing to do with Ted's death. I've got nothing more to tell you, so for Christ's sake leave me in peace to get on with my work." He started chopping pork ribs with violence. "Go on. Bugger off," he added.

"Have you got the cuffs there, constable?" Watkins asked. Reluctantly Evan produced the handcuffs.

"I don't want to have to do this, Gareth," he said to Evans-the-Meat. "Why don't you just come quietly, eh?"

"I tell you I didn't do it!" Evans-the-Meat yelled. "I'm not going anywhere. I know my rights. You can't touch me without my lawyer being present."

"You'll get a chance to talk to your lawyer soon enough, I expect," Watkins said. He took a step toward Evans-the-Meat with the handcuffs open and ready. Evans-the-Meat's eyes darted around the room like a trapped animal. "No!" he yelled. "You're not handcuffing me!" His hand half raised the meat cleaver.

"What seems to be taking so long, sergeant?" D.I. Hughes' crisp voice made them all start. He stood in the doorway eyeing the butcher with distaste. "Resisting arrest, is he? Foolish move. Put the cuffs on him and then drive him straight down to HQ, Watkins. I'll talk to him there."

Evans-the-Meat lowered his arm and went limp, like a deflating balloon. He looked down in horror as the cuffs were snapped onto his wrists. "Don't do that," he pleaded. "What will my customers think if they see me taken off to jail? You know what people are like. I'll lose all my trade. I'm an upright citizen. Ask Constable Evans. He'll tell you, won't you, Evan bach?"

"Don't make it worse for yourself, Gareth," Evan muttered. "Just go down there and answer their questions. If you're innocent, you've got nothing to worry about."

"Oh no? I've heard how the police get confessions out of people when they've got them alone in a cell. Torture chambers, that's what they've got down in Caernarfon. Don't let them take me down there, Evan. You've got to help me, man."

Evan winced as Evans-the-Meat was crammed into the backseat of Sergeant Watkins' squad car. Evan could hear him yelling as the car drove off. He felt slightly sick.

Chapter 15

Evan sat at his desk and stared at the wall. After the morning's activity the silence was oppressive. He couldn't forget the butcher's panic stricken face and still felt in some way responsible for letting him down.

At last he got up and went outside. A brisk wind was blowing from the high peaks, sending clouds like puffballs across the sky. Evan glanced at his watch. It was well past lunchtime but he no longer felt hungry. Having missed his breakfast, he had been starving by midmorning and had to get a couple of packets of crisps from Roberts-the-Pump's snack bar. If he went home now, he knew that Mrs. Williams would have a gargantuan plate of food congealing in the oven for him, and she'd be waiting to ply him with questions, too.

On impulse he climbed over the style and started up the sheep path to Owens' farm. The wind blew in his face and snatched his breath away but he kept on climbing steadily until he had passed the farmhouse and the village lay below him. How neat and tidy it all looked from here, he thought. You'd never think it was a place where murders took place.

None of the events of the past few days made sense—a stranger breaking into Annie's house and stealing a gun that killed another man who had just moved here. An old colonel being hit over the head after he discovered an ancient ruin, and Evans-the-Meat taken to jail as the prime suspect.

Evan sank down onto a large rock. It was covered with gray-green traces of lichen and warm in the sun. He wished that Bronwen were up there with him. When he talked things through with her, he was able to see them more clearly. But Bronwen was teaching school and he was alone, looking through a complete fog.

Evans-the-Meat. That's where he should start. Why was he so sure that the butcher hadn't killed Ted Morgan? He had threatened to. He had even tried to. He had admitted going to the bungalow. And if that little gun had been the only weapon available, why couldn't he have picked it up in a fit of rage and pulled the trigger? But how would he have got hold of Annie's gun in the first place? How would he even have known Annie owned a gun?

Evan's gaze swept the hillside, then he suddenly froze. Someone was climbing up the path toward him, moving quickly. From the long skirt that billowed out behind her, it could only be one person. It must be some sort of emergency, Evan thought. They had sent her to find him. He got to his feet.

"What is it, Bron?" he called.

She started in surprise. "Do you make a habit of rearing up from behind rocks, Evan Evans?" she asked with a nervous laugh. "You almost made my heart jump out of my throat."

"I'm sorry. I thought you must be looking for me."

"Looking for you?"

"I thought they'd sent you to get me because something had happened." Evan felt his face flushing. "Aren't you supposed to be in school?" he added. "It is Tuesday, isn't it?"

Bronwen smiled at his confusion. "Half-day holiday for

146

parent conferences. I'm supposed to be down there, going through report cards, but I had to take a quick break."

"Funny, I was just thinking about you," Evan said.

"That's nice." Bronwen's cornflower blue eyes met his.

Evan nodded. "I was thinking how I'm always able to see things more clearly when I can talk them through with you."

Bronwen sat on the rock. "Alright. Try me."

"You're supposed to be meeting parents."

"Not for an hour." She patted the rock beside her. "Come on. Sit down. I'd like to help, if I can."

Evan sat. "I suppose you heard that Ted Morgan was killed this morning?"

Bronwen nodded. "And that they took away Evans-the-Meat, hollering and yelling."

Evan sighed. "He was the obvious suspect. Everyone saw him threaten to kill Ted last night."

"But you don't think he did?"

"I didn't think so," Evan said. "Now I'm not so sure. I was just thinking—what do I really know about him, apart from being a rabid Welsh nationalist and having a hot temper and liking good beer?"

"Why did you think he hadn't killed Ted Morgan?" Bronwen asked. "Just loyalty?"

Evan shook his head. "It wasn't his type of crime. A little pearl handled revolver. A bullet between the eyes?"

"You think Evans-the-Meat would have cut him in half with the cleaver?" Bronwen suggested. "Or throttled him with his bare hands?"

"More likely," Evan agreed. "And only when he was good and drunk and his temper was up. Not later, when he'd cooled down. But now I'm wondering, Bron. Annie Pigeon reported a prowler. What if that was Evans-the-Meat? He told me his wife is away a lot. What if he is the kind of man who peeps through windows at attractive women?"

147

"It would be easy enough to slip from his place to her back yard through the bushes," Bronwen agreed. "But surely people would know. Everyone knows everything in a place like this."

"Maybe it's just Annie he's after," Evan said. "A sexy woman suddenly arrives in Llanfair when his wife is away? She's the type that turns heads."

"So I've noticed," Bronwen said dryly.

Evan ignored the comment and went on. "And maybe Annie wasn't quite telling the truth when she said that she'd forgotten about the gun."

"The gun? It belonged to that woman?"

"She said she'd forgotten she owned it. She suggested the prowler must have found it when he broke in. But I'm wondering if she didn't take it out when Evans-the-Meat was watching, so that he knew where to find it when he needed a weapon to kill Ted Morgan."

"It's possible," Bronwen agreed.

"The one thing that doesn't make sense is the colonel."

Bronwen looked up, surprised. "The colonel?"

"Evans-the-Meat would never have killed him, would he?"

Bronwen's eyes opened even wider. "You're saying that the colonel was killed? We all thought it was an accident."

"We kept quiet about it until now. We didn't want to alarm anybody. But someone hit the colonel over the head and pushed him into the river."

"And you don't think Evans-the-Meat could have done that?"

Evan shook his head. "He liked the colonel, didn't he? Besides, he was excited that the colonel had just discovered the site of an ancient ruin and that Llanfair might soon have its own historical monument."

"But he didn't want more tourism, remember."

"That's not a strong enough reason to kill the colonel. He might have wanted to stop Ted Morgan's theme park, but that was different." He paused, trying to remember clearly. "Besides," he added, "Evans-the-Meat couldn't have killed the colonel. He was in the pub long after the colonel left. I'd swear to that."

"Which must mean that there are two killers, within two days, in a little place like Llanfair. That doesn't seem likely." Bronwen pushed her hair out from her face and started to get to her feet. "I'm sorry, but I really should be heading back. My first appointment is at two-thirty. Freddie Price's mother. I've got to find a way to tell her politely that she spoils her son."

Evan smiled and stood up too. "We've all got our own problems. I'll walk down with you."

They started down the trail.

"So what are you going to do?" Bronwen asked over her shoulder.

"I don't know. As Sergeant Watkins said, if I want to remove Evans-the-Meat from the prime suspect list, I've got to come up with someone better."

"Like who?"

Evan shrugged. "The ones who benefit from Ted Morgan's death are his sister and brother-in-law. But they didn't even know the colonel. And they didn't know Annie Pigeon and they didn't know that she owned a gun."

"What makes you so sure that you're looking for a local person?" Bronwen asked. "If both the colonel and Ted Morgan came from London, why wouldn't their killer have come from there too? I'd get the London police to start looking into their lives down there."

"The D.I. has already started that ball rolling," Evan said. "All this has nothing to do with me, really. I found the bodies and called in the detectives. Now I'm supposed to go back to being the village bobby and mind my own business."

"But you're not going to, are you?" Bronwen flashed him a challenging smile.

"I'd like to find out the truth for myself," Evan admitted.

They had reached the path leading to the schoolhouse. Bronwen paused. "I'll help any way I can. You know that, Evan."

"Thanks, Bron. See you then."

"I'm looking forward to Saturday."

"Saturday?" For a second his mind was blank.

"The Italian restaurant. Don't tell me you'd already forgotten. Our first real date?" She looked hurt.

"Oh no. I hadn't forgotten. It's just I've had so much on my mind, these past few days. The Italian restaurant—that will be nice."

"You sound as if it's a visit to the dentist," Bronwen chided.

"No, really. I'm looking forward to it too," Evan insisted. "I'll look out my good suit."

Bronwen laughed. "The one you only wear for funerals? It's just dinner, Evan. Nothing more serious."

She tossed her long braid over her shoulder and strode out toward the back gate of the schoolhouse. Evan smiled as he watched her go. This reluctance to get involved with a woman again was stupid, he told himself. It was about time he got out there and started enjoying life. Forget about a murder investigation that was none of his business . . .

He was glad when the clock ticked around to opening time at the Red Dragon. There had been no more word from HQ and Evans-the-Meat hadn't reappeared. Evan hoped the butcher hadn't got himself into deeper trouble with his loose tongue. For once he had a good excuse for going to the pub. Most of the other men would be there and one of them might know something. One of them might even be the murderer, and murderers were supposed to be cocky, weren't they? They enjoyed talking about the crime and asking how the police were coming along in their investigation. Evan would be alert for any of that.

The main bar was almost empty. Betsy was standing alone, lost in thought. She was dressed, for once, in a simple flowery dress with short sleeves. A shaft of sunlight was falling on her, giving her an aura of innocence and purity which she didn't often possess. Evan stood for a second, watching her. Maybe he had been too hasty in deciding that she wasn't his type.

As if sensing his eyes on her, Betsy looked up and smiled. "Rough day, eh, Evan bach?" She began filling a pint mug without being asked. "Here, get this inside you. It will make a new man of you, although I can't say that there was much wrong with the old one," she added, her eyes travelling over him with approval.

"Thanks, love. Cheers," Evan said, draining half the mug of McAffrey's in one swallow. "I needed that."

"Everyone's been talking about it," Betsy went on. "No one can rightly believe it. Ted Morgan—he seemed like a chap who was full of himself, didn't he? I've been looked at by enough men to know when a chap thinks he's hot stuff. And that's how Ted Morgan looked at me—even though he was almost old enough to be my father and I'd never have gone out with him anyway, even if he was rich."

Evan drained the rest of the glass. "It doesn't look as though he did pull the trigger himself."

"That's what I was wondering. I hear they took poor old Evans-the-Meat away for questioning. What do they think he might have to do with it?"

"He did try to throttle Ted Morgan in full view of everyone last night."

"Oh that? That's just Evans-the-Meat. You know how he is. All hot air, but harmless really, isn't he? They should know that. Same again?" she took the glass without waiting for an answer and began to fill it. "I just hope he doesn't act daft and start saying things he'll regret later," she went on. "You know, like threatening to kill the Queen of England or accusing the inspector of being an Englishman."

Evan smiled. "You're right. He can be a bloody fool at times, can't he? But you don't think he could really kill someone, do you?"

"By mistake, maybe, but I don't see him going up to someone's house and shooting them."

"Somebody did."

"I don't know why they're looking here," Betsy said. "I mean, none of us knew Ted Morgan, did we? He went away before I was born and I don't think he's kept in touch with any of the people around here. Who knows what he had been doing for twenty years?"

Evan nodded.

"Probably some disgruntled woman that he walked out on," Betsy said. "He was a flirt, alright. He looked at me like he wanted to undress me, if you know what I mean. What's the betting she followed him here and gave him what he deserved."

"Have you noticed any disgruntled women wandering about Llanfair?" Evan chuckled. "Someone would have seen her."

"Not necessarily," Betsy said with a knowing look. "It was the night of the big meeting, remember? Everyone was at the hall. Anyone could have come into the village, gone up to Ted Morgan's cottage, and waited for him there. There were lots of strange cars parked and people driving away, weren't there?"

"Betsy, you know, you should have been a detective," Evan said.

"I'd settle for marrying one some day."

"Do you want me to ask Sergeant Watkins if there are any single blokes down at HQ?"

Betsy made a face. "If I weren't working here, I'd throw

152

this glass all over you," she said. "You can't keep running for ever, Evan Evans."

"I have enough complications in my life right now without worrying about women," Evan said.

"Then you should go up to London and see who had a real reason to kill Ted Morgan," Betsy said.

"How can I? I'm not a member of the C.I.D. I'm the community police officer for Llanfair district, nothing more."

"There's nothing to stop you from doing some snooping in your spare time, is there?"

Evan grinned. "Maybe you're right."

"And if you felt like taking someone with you to London . . . someone who's been dying to see a West End show and do some shopping in Oxford Street?"

"I'll see if Sergeant Watkins is free this weekend," Evan finished for her.

This time she threw an ice cube at him. Evan dodged and nearly backed into someone who had just come in. "Oh, Annie, I'm sorry. I didn't see you there," he muttered. "I was being attacked."

"So I saw," Annie said. "I can't stay. I left the little one watching the telly, but I saw you going into the pub and I wanted to buy you a drink, to thank you for all you've done for me."

"Me? It was nothing, Annie. I was just doing my job." Evan was beginning to feel hot and uncomfortable. He was very aware of Betsy's critical stare.

"Oh you did far more than that and you know it," Annie went on. "You've been such a comfort to me, to know that you're there, just in case."

"In case what?"

"I need protecting, I suppose," she said simply. "I thought I could get along just fine without a man in my life, but there are times when it's good to have a big, strong bloke around."

"Can I get you something, miss?" Betsy asked in Welsh.

Annie looked blank.

"She doesn't speak Welsh, Betsy," Evan said. "She's just moved here."

"She'd better learn in a hurry if she wants to know what people are saying, hadn't she?" Betsy said, also in Welsh.

Evan turned to Annie. "She was asking what you were drinking, and I'm paying, by the way."

"But I wanted to treat you."

"Treat him to what?" Betsy muttered in Welsh.

"I won't hear of it," Evan said.

Annie gave him a dazzling smile. "I do like a man who's forceful and masterly. Thanks then, I'll have a quick lager and lime."

"A lager and quicklime?" Betsy asked with the barest hint of a smile.

Evan decided there was nothing wrong with Betsy's brain. She might act like a dumb blonde sometimes, but her wit was sharp enough when needed. She poured the drink and Evan handed it to Annie.

"Have you got time to sit for a minute?" Evan asked.

She glanced at the door. "I really shouldn't leave her too long, but we could sit by the window, couldn't we, so I could keep an eye on the front door. I told her not to move until I get back. She should be fine."

She led the way to the table in the window and sat down.

"I was that shook up today," she said. "Finding out that my gun was missing and knowing what they'd think. I felt so stupid that it didn't cross my mind before, but honestly, I don't think I even remember seeing it when I unpacked. I just shoved all my undies into the drawer and the gun must have been with them."

"What if it wasn't?" Evan asked. "What if someone had taken it before you moved? Is that possible?"

"Who would do that?"

"I thought you might be able to tell me."

154

Annie shook her head. "No one that I can think of. I was staying with a girlfriend. I told you, I hadn't even thought about that gun for years. But it was lucky that I thought I heard a prowler, wasn't it? Or you'd never have been at my house all evening and they might have suspected me." She took a sip of her drink. "But I hear they already got the bloke that did it. Do you reckon he was the one who broke in when you and I were on our little walk on Sunday?"

"I've no idea," Evan said. "They took fingerprints from your cottage today, didn't they? We'll just have to see if any of them match."

"Llanfair for peace and quiet. Who'd have thought it." Annie laughed loudly. She drained the glass. "Oh well. Must run, I suppose. But I've got another bottle of wine in the fridge. You could always stop by later, if you wanted."

Evan was conscious of his instructions to encourage the friendship with Annie. "I'll see if I have time," he said.

"Thanks for the drink. You're a real gent," Annie said, getting up. "Say good-bye to her behind the bar for me, will you? I don't know how to say it in Welsh."

The next morning Betsy was up early and saw Bronwen standing in the middle of the school playground surrounded by her pupils. She took a deep breath then went up to her.

"Bronwen Price, you and I have to talk," Betsy said.

Bronwen looked around at all the eager little faces.

"Not now, Betsy. It's time for them to get in lines." She clapped her hands. "In lines, everybody. No pushing, Gwillum. No running now."

With much scuffling the children formed themselves into two lines: boys and girls.

"Soon, Bronwen. We have to talk soon." Betsy followed Bronwen as she walked to the head of the line. "Or it may be too late."

Bronwen looked up with interest. "Too late for what?"

"Us. You and me. I never thought I'd be on your side, but we Llanfair girls have got to stick together."

"Over what?"

"Have you seen that woman yet?"

"The one who's just moved in?"

"The one who is making a beeline for Evan."

Bronwen flushed. "Evan would never—"

"Yes he would," Betsy insisted. "You know how willing he is and how naïve too. She's fluttering her eyelashes and saying how grateful she is for his help and he's lapping it up."

Bronwen laughed nervously. "You know Evan. He just likes to be helpful."

"She invited him to her house for a glass of wine again last night and he didn't say no. I was listening."

Bronwen could see the children were getting restless. "Alright everybody. Lead into the classroom. No pushing. No talking. Off you go, Sian, ladies first."

The two lines of children began to file into the school. Bronwen glanced back at Betsy. "I don't know what you think we can do."

"Something," Betsy said. "we can't just stand here and watch that woman get her claws into him, can we?"

"I think you're overreacting, Betsy," Bronwen said. "Evan's not stupid. If he says he's only trying to be helpful, then he is."

"But don't you see that's how she'll hook him," Betsy hissed as the last child passed into the classroom. "Men feel important when they're needed. She had him help her put the little kid to bed the other night—I heard her say so. You don't want him getting to like the daddy role, do you?"

Bronwen looked at her thoughtfully. "So what do you think we should do? I'm not about to play the helpless female myself to lure him back."

"Of course not," Betsy said. "What you must do, Bronwen Price, is to start dressing sexier."

156

Bronwen was so surprised that she laughed. "Me? Dress sexier?"

"Of course. You've got to compete with her, haven't you? Look at those jeans she was wearing—looked like they'd been painted onto her, didn't they? And look at you in all those skirts—you'd never even know you'd got legs under there."

"But that's just me, Betsy. It's the way I am. Evan knows that."

She started to move toward the schoolhouse door. "I have to go in. I can't leave them alone in there."

"Think about it, Bronwen Price," Betsy said. "Men like to see a bit of flesh occasionally. I do my best in that department, but it seems that Evan Evans has got a eye for you right now. And I'd rather you got him than that outsider, so I'm prepared to help, if I can. I could lend you some clothes, if you like. I've got a lovely neon-green spandex top with a low neck, or a see-through blouse, or how about a strapless sundress. You're welcome to come over and try them on anytime."

Bronwen gave another nervous laugh. "You're very kind, Betsy, but I can't see myself in spandex somehow."

"You don't want to lose him to her, do you?" Betsy demanded.

"No, of course not," Bronwen flushed.

"Then think about it. And maybe you should find yourself another bloke, just to make him jealous. That usually works like a charm."

"Betsy I'm not the type who plays little games. If Evan doesn't like me as I am, then he's not the one for me anyway."

"Fine, if that's how you want it," Betsy said, "But I'm not giving up without a fight. I've sent for one of those black push-up bras from a catalogue. See yer, Bronwen."

She gave Bronwen a friendly wave and ran off across the school playground. Bronwen turned and went into the schoolroom. Ridiculous, she thought. Betsy obviously meant well, but neon spandex? Bronwen had to laugh at the thought. All the same, she sometimes wondered whether Evan actually thought of her as a woman or just another village buddy. Maybe she would buy a new dress for that date on Saturday— not neon spandex, but a little more form-fitting.

Chapter 16

Evan was on his way to the police station when his pager went. He hurried the last few yards to his office and returned Sergeant Watkins' call.

"Bad news, Evan. You were wrong about your butcher friend."

"Evans-the-Meat? Did he confess to something?"

"Worse than that. They found his print on the doorway. He didn't just stand there outside and then go home again. That's enough for the D.I. He's booked him for the murder. Case closed as far as he's concerned."

"But what about the colonel? How does he explain that?"

"We haven't got that far yet."

"He didn't kill the colonel, sarge. He couldn't have. I was there in the pub. I saw Evans-the-Meat there after the colonel had left."

"So you think we're looking for another killer altogether?"

"Or you've got the wrong man." Evan took a deep breath. "Listen, sarge, I've been thinking about taking a little trip to London, maybe this weekend. Any interest in going along with me?"

"Strictly off the record, you mean?"

159

"For me, yes. You could probably get permission, couldn't you? Someone needs to check into the colonel's life there, since we know for sure that Evans-the-Meat didn't kill him."

"That's true enough. The D.I.'s in a good mood this morning with all his fingerprint success. I'll ask him if I can have Friday off. I'd quite like to be away this weekend, in fact. The wife wants the kitchen redecorated. She was talking about going to wallpaper shops, and you know how much I enjoy that."

Evan chuckled, then grew serious again. "About these fingerprints, sarge. Did Evans' fingerprints show up on the gun?"

"No, but the D.I. reckons he tried to wipe it or he held it with a handkerchief. It's partially wiped clean."

"So Evans was stupid enough to touch the door on his way in and then wipe the gun clean?"

"That's what the D.I. thinks."

"And what do you think?"

"I'm . . . keeping an open mind for the moment. Having met the bloke, I'm inclined to go along with you—it's not his kind of crime."

"Any other interesting fingerprints in the room?"

"Plenty. The house was let by the week, wasn't it? But the only prints on the gun are the victim's and your friend Annie's. And we know she couldn't have shot him because she was with you. They're trying to run a check on her background, by the way. And she's a hard one to trace. You just better pray that she doesn't have some kind of criminal connection—the D.I. read way more into your friendship than you'd like."

"She hasn't told me a thing," Evan said. "I've dropped enough hints, but she's stayed tight-lipped."

"That must be frustrating for you." Watkins chuckled.

"Give me a break, sarge. Not you as well. To me Annie Pigeon is one of my responsibilities in Llanfair, the same as Evans-the-Meat."

"But easier on the eye, right?" Watkins laughed. "I'll call

160

you to let you know whether it's on for this weekend then. If the D.I. okays it, then he picks up the tab."

"In which case we stay at the Dorchester!"

"And if not, we stay at a boardinghouse in Clapham."

"Fine with me," Evan said. "I just want to feel that I'm doing something positive. It's hanging around here feeling helpless that I can't stand."

"I'll see if I can get permission to take you with me, officially," Watkins said. "After all, you were the one who knew the colonel. It might be useful to have you there. And the wife would be happier if I had someone to keep an eye on me."

"To make sure you don't visit the girlie clubs?" Evan chuckled.

"To make sure I don't get lost," Watkins confessed. "She doesn't have a very high opinion of my map-reading skills. Ever since the time I wouldn't ask directions on the way home from Liverpool and we wound up in Scotland."

Evan laughed as he hung up the phone. He had to agree with Betsy that Ted Morgan's killer was more likely to be someone who had known him recently and that meant someone in London. Betsy was a sharp girl. In fact, if Bronwen hadn't been around—he broke his thought off in horror. Bronwen! He had a date with Bronwen on Saturday night. Now he'd have to postpone it. He just hoped she'd be understanding.

Bronwen smiled to herself as she rode the bus up from Bangor. She had been to the new shopping center and actually found a dress she liked. It was far from Betsy's neon spandex idea of what was sexy but it was definitely right. It was sleeveless, blue denim, the top embroidered with tiny flowers and very form-hugging when tied back at the waist. It matched her eyes perfectly and made her look tall and slim. It also complemented her healthy outdoor look that new woman definitely didn't have.

161

Bronwen was horrified to find herself thinking in terms of rivalry, but she couldn't help it. Betsy had confirmed her own suspicions. The woman was definitely after Evan. Bronwen had observed her and it was all true. She was trying to lure him through her daughter and her sexy clothes. And he didn't seem to be fighting too hard, either. Twice Bronwen had seen her approach him and twice he had gone with her.

But after the date this Saturday, everything would be alright. They'd have a wonderful intimate dinner, they'd talk and laugh a lot, the way they always did. Maybe she could even persuade him to take a romantic latenight stroll along the seafront. He'd realize how much he enjoyed her company. She'd make him realize how much they had in common and the new woman would be history.

Wrapped up in these warm, exciting thoughts, she was startled to see Evan coming out of the school yard as she walked up the street from the bus stop.

"Oh, there you are, Bron. I was looking for you," he said. He definitely looked worried. It must be a strain, carrying on a murder investigation, Bronwen thought.

"I was down in Bangor, shopping. How's your investigation coming along?"

"Not going anywhere at the moment," Evan said. "I'm stumped on this one, Bron."

"Maybe we can talk it through some more on Saturday. Two heads are better than one, aren't they?"

Evan's face fell. "About Saturday," he said. "I'm afraid we'll have to postpone our date."

"I see." Bronwen's face was a mask of stone.

"We could do it next weekend, maybe?"

"I might be busy next weekend," Bronwen said. "There are some friends I might go hiking with—old friends from university I haven't seen for a while. I'll have to get back to you on that."

"Okay," Evan said. "Some other time then."

"Maybe. It depends."

"On what?"

"A lot of things." Bronwen walked calmly past Evan toward the schoolhouse. Evan watched her go. Something was going on here he didn't quite understand.

Chapter 17

"Now I know why I don't come to London more often," Sergeant Watkins said as they fought their way through the crowds inside Paddington Station. A large woman almost knocked him flying with her luggage cart. "Too many bloody people and all of them in a hurry."

Evan nodded. "I grew up in Swansea, which I always thought of as a big city, but it's nothing compared to this."

They came out into smoggy sunlight. Buses roared past, taxis honked, the lights changed, and a solid mass of people streamed across the street. Evan and Watkins stood there, looking and feeling like a pair of country bumpkins.

"Where first?" Watkins asked. "Check into the hotel, do you think?"

"We don't want to carry around these bags, do we?" Evan agreed.

"So we need the taxi rank."

"Does the North Wales police spring for taxis?" Evan asked. "There's the tube station right there."

"When we're carrying luggage, it does," Watkins said firmly. He glanced down at the small sports bag in his hand. "And to me this counts as luggage."

164

"Okay, after we've checked in, do we go to the colonel's flat?" Evan suggested.

"Maybe we should start off with Ted Morgan," Watkins said thoughtfully as they joined the line for taxis. "If we want to check on his business contacts, they probably won't be in the city tomorrow. They'll have gone home to their country estates for the weekend."

"Good thinking, sarge," Evan said.

"The address we have for him isn't too far from our hotel, is it?" Watkins asked.

"It's Mayfair and the hotel is near Victoria. I don't know about walking distance."

"I thought you were the one who tramped over all those bloody hills."

"That's different. Pavements are hard on the feet and I've got my good shoes on."

Watkins chuckled.

"Funny, that, about his address," Evan said thoughtfully.

"What's funny?"

"That the only address we could find for him was the one his father had." He looked at Watkins. "If you were a businessman, wouldn't you carry cards everywhere with you? And yet he had nothing with him—no paperwork, no cards, nothing at all to do with his business in London."

"Perhaps he wanted to get away from it all?"

Evan shook his head. "Successful businessmen never want to get away from it all. They take their cell phone and their electronic diaries."

"Yes, maybe you've got something there."

They reached the head of the queue.

"Where to, mates?" the taxi driver asked cheerfully.

"The Buckingham Arms Hotel," Watkins said, climbing in. "Do you know it?"

"Yeah. Down near Victoria, ain't it?"

"What's it like?"

165

"Well, it ain't no Buckingham Palace," the cable said. "But yer gets what yer pays for, don't yer."

"And in the case of the North Wales police, they don't pay much," Watkins commented to Evan.

The taxi took them down the Edgeware Road and past Marble Arch.

"The missus loves this kind of thing," Watkins commented, peering out at Speakers' Corner, the Dorchester Hotel, and then horsemen riding, turned out in traditional bowler hats and hacking jackets, through Hyde Park. "She was really put out that I was going to London and not taking her. She said she'd been dying to take our Tiffany and show her the sights and this would be a perfect opportunity. I had to tell her that the officer I was going with was a stickler for rules and would report me if she came along."

"Thanks a lot, sarge."

"Sorry, old son. It was that or have the wife and Tiffany wanting money for Harrods and the theatre."

"I think you owe me a beer for that," Evan said.

"I wouldn't mind a beer right now. It's muggy isn't it, and it was hot in that train, too. But I suppose work has to come first. You've got the map. Look up how we get to the street in Mayfair. We'll drop off our bags and then start checking on Mr. Ted Morgan."

Evan had just located Ted Morgan's address in Mayfair as the cab pulled up outside a row of tall Victorian houses behind Victoria Station. The Buckingham Arms was one of several that had been converted into hotels.

"He's right," Watkins muttered to Evan. "It's not Buckingham Palace. It's not even as impressive as the hotels on the esplanade at Llandudno."

"It shows how highly the North Wales police values you, sarge," Evan said as he got out of the cab after the sergeant.

They signed in and got two keys from an uninterested Ger-

166

man girl at the front desk and then climbed the four flights to their rooms. There was no elevator. The rooms were small and spartan and looked out on the railway tracks. They came straight down again without bothering to unpack and took another cab back to Mayfair.

"Posh, isn't it?" Watkins said as they stood outside an elegant glass-and-marble fronted building squeezed between Georgian houses on a quiet square just behind Park Lane. "I reckon Mr. Morgan did alright for himself. Let's go and see if anyone's at home."

The front door opened with a remote buzzer and they found themselves at a glass fronted reception desk. A young girl with pouty red lips and fake eyelashes was filing long red fingernails.

"We're looking for suite 2B. Mr. Ted Morgan," Sergeant Watkins said. "Is anyone in residence at the moment?"

"Mr. Morgan isn't here," the girl said in a bored voice. The upper class veneer to her voice couldn't quite hide its cockney undertones.

Watkins produced an ID card. "We're police officers. Can you show us the suite, please."

"There's no suite," she said. "Mr. Morgan doesn't live here. We just hold his mail for him."

"Then do you have his real address?"

"No, we don't."

"You don't have any way of contacting him?"

"No. He sends someone in to get the mail once a week."

"What about recently?"

"Nobody's been in for a while. In fact our last bill hasn't been paid."

"So his mail has been piling up. May we see it?"

She looked at him defiantly. "Nothing's come except junk mail and we thow that away."

"So he's had no letters at all recently? No bills?"

The cold defiant look didn't waver. "I told you, didn't I."

"You're telling me you don't know his real business address? You don't have any contact address at all for him?"

"I told you. I don't know anything."

"And you're sure there are no letters waiting for him?"

"No." She gave them a cold, insolent stare.

"We're police officers, you know. We could come back with a search warrant," Watkins said angrily.

"Come back with what you like. Turn the place upside down. You won't find anything here. We just held his mail."

"I'm afraid she was telling the truth, sarge," Evan said as they closed the front door behind them. "What's the betting he just used that address to impress people like his father."

"That would explain why no letters have come for a few weeks. So what now?"

"We could try looking him up in the phone book."

"He's hardly going to answer, is he?" Watkins chuckled.

"No, but somebody might. I got the feeling he was a ladies' man. He could have had a live-in."

"Alright. Let's find a phone booth." He glanced back at the building they had just left. "I don't think that young lady would offer us the use of her phone somehow."

Evan smiled. "We need to find out where he lived so that we can talk to the neighbors."

"And we need to find where he worked too. He must have made his money somehow, so he must have a business address somewhere. And he had to have held a business license. That would tell us if he was operating under a fictitious name."

"All that information would be on his tax forms too, wouldn't it?" Evan suggested.

"Oh yes, don't worry. We'll catch up with him somehow," Watkins said confidently as they reached a phone booth.

"Here we are, Evans. Write these down," Watkins said,

scanning the phone book. "There are three Edward Morgans in greater London."

Evan scribbled down the numbers and Watkins dialled the first number. "Mr. Edward Morgan?" he asked as the phone was picked up.

"Yeah? What do yer want?" a harsh cockney voice demanded.

"Obviously not him," Watkins muttered as he replaced the receiver. "Still very much alive and kicking."

The next phone call was answered by Mrs. Edward Morgan who said her husband was at work and said they could get hold of him at the London Transport garage. He drove a number 32 bus.

"Of course, our Ted Morgan might not live in London. He'd probably live out in the commuter belt in one of those pseudotudors," Evan commented as Watkins dialled the third number. "They wouldn't be in this book."

"Hello?" The accent was definitely Welsh.

"Mrs. Morgan?" Watkins motioned for Evan to be quiet. "I wondered if I could talk to your husband."

"Oh, but he's not here at the moment. He's away on business."

"Where, exactly?"

"I'm not rightly sure," she said. "He travels a lot."

"Has he been away long?"

"About a month now. Has there been some kind of trouble?"

"I couldn't say," Watkins said. "We're from the North Wales police, trying to trace a Mr. Edward Morgan. Maybe we could come round to see you?"

"I suppose so. Nothing's happened to Eddy, has it? He was right as rain when he called last weekend."

The house was a typical semidetached on an ordinary street in Ealing. Nicely kept but humble. Mrs. Morgan was ordinary-looking too: chubby, middle-aged, and wearing a floral print polyester dress. "Please come inside," she said, her face a mask of fear. "It's not bad news, is it? I always hate it when he goes off on these sales trips like this and I don't hear from him."

"Are you from Wales then, Mrs. Morgan?" Sergeant Watkins asked as she showed them into a neat little sitting room with a plush blue three-piece suite and a telly in the corner.

"Oh yes. We're both from Wales, but I'm from south and Eddy's from north. We tease each other about it—about which part is better, you know."

"Do you have a recent photo of your husband, Mrs. Morgan?" Evan asked gently.

"Oh, yes. Here's one on the mantelpiece, taken at our Sandra's wedding," she said with pride in her voice. She handed it to the policemen. They found themselves looking at a large, round, balding man, standing beside a rather plain girl in a white wedding dress.

Evan handed back the photo. "I'm sorry to have troubled you," he said, "but it's not the man we're looking for."

"You mean he's alright?" A big smile spread across her face. "Oh, what a relief. You've made my day."

"It takes all types, doesn't it," Watkins muttered to Evan as they went back to the Ealing Broadway tube station.

Evan looked up enquiringly.

"I mean that Mr. Morgan was no oil painting, but she looked as if you'd told her she'd won the pools when you said he was alright. It just proves there's someone for everyone in this world."

"But we're no nearer to finding Ted Morgan's real address," Evan said. "Would the Greater London Council hold the business licenses?"

By the time government offices were closing, they had failed to find any trace of Ted Morgan's existence. No business license

170

had been issued to him. He paid no tax on property in any of the London boroughs. A call to Newcastle failed to find him in an initial income tax search. It was as if Ted Morgan didn't exist.

"So where do we go from here, sarge?" Evan asked.

They were sitting at an outdoor table at a pub called the Grapes in Shepherd Market with pints of beer in front of them.

"Don't ask me, I haven't a clue." He took a big gulp of beer. "Bloody watery London beer. Not a patch on Brains."

"He must live somewhere, mustn't he?" Evan said. "And he must have made money somehow. He was expensively dressed. He drove a nice car."

"Damn," Sergeant Watkins said. "We should have traced the registration on the car. We'll try to do that tomorrow, if anyone works on Saturdays these days."

"We could also contact Scotland Yard and see if they've got any kind of file on him."

"Why do you think that?"

"I'm thinking that a man who could afford nice things had to have some sort of income, and if we can't trace it, it has to be illegal."

"Or he had a rich girlfriend to keep him."

"That's a possibility too, but I don't know how we'd ever trace her."

"We could make sure all the London papers publish the news of his murder and see who comes out of the woodwork. If he was rich, I'd imagine there would be interested parties wanting to get their share. Possibly people he owes money to as well."

"So we check with Scotland Yard in the morning, then we get in touch with the newspapers," Evan said, jotting it down in his notebook. "Now I'm beginning to wonder whether he really lived in London at all. Maybe he just wanted to look like a bigshot to his dad and the people at home and he was really working somewhere humble like Stoke on Trent."

"The car registration should help," Watkins said. "I think I'll call HQ on that right now."

Evan looked around him, taking in the fashionable London clothes and listening to conversations as commuters gathered for afterwork drinks. He found it hard to follow their conversations, and not just because they were speaking English with London accents. The group of young, casually dressed men next to him peppered their conversation with words like gigabytes and Web sites, making Evan, who didn't yet own a computer, feel that English wasn't the only foreign language being spoken here. The group of dark-suited young women was talking about networking and promos and launches. It really was a different world here, he decided.

He had just finished his beer when Watkins came back. "That was a bloody waste of time. It was leased to Ted Morgan Productions, address at his dad's farm, and he paid cash. So we're none the wiser."

"Maybe we should forget about Ted for a while and concentrate on the colonel first," Evan said. "At least we have an address for him. Let's go and visit his flat in the morning. Then we can go to Scotland Yard and find out if they know anything we don't know about Ted Morgan."

"And what do you fancy doing tonight?" Watkins asked. "A slap-up dinner, a show, a nightclub?"

"Is the North Wales police paying?"

"If we base our activities on what the North Wales police is paying, it's McDonald's or fish and chips followed by a look at the lights in Piccadilly Circus."

In the end they settled for an Indian restaurant just behind Victoria Station where they had a meal of lamb biriani and tandoori chicken before returning to the Buckingham Arms Hotel.

"At least it's clean, I suppose you can say that for it," Watkins commented as they walked up four flights of stairs to their rooms. "And I could do with the exercise to walk off all those chapattis."

"I just wish they hadn't made the rooms for thin people," Evan said. "My room is so narrow that there's no space beside the bed to get dressed."

"I suppose it discourages visitors and hanky-panky." Watkins laughed.

"It certainly does," Evan agreed. "There's no way two people would ever fit in one of these rooms, let alone these beds."

As he closed his door behind him, he found himself thinking about Bronwen. Was she angry about his breaking their date, or didn't she even care that much? Would she rather spend a weekend with friends from university than with him? He just wished he knew what was going on inside her head, and what he really felt about her.

Chapter 18

Their hotel redeemed itself in Evan's eyes by producing a hearty, if cholesterol-laden, English breakfast down in a dark basement room. The three strips of lean bacon, the fat juicy sausage, two eggs, fried bread, and grilled tomatoes were not quite up to Mrs. Williams standard but they would definitely keep him going all day.

"My wife's not going to like this," Sergeant Watkins said, patting his stomach. "She's always onto me to watch my weight."

"You'll just have to make sure you walk it off today, sarge," Evan said. "And we can start by walking to the colonel's place in Kensington."

"Kensington? Isn't that bloody miles?"

"We can go through the park. It will do you good."

Sergeant Watkins sighed. "I don't know why I brought you along. You're a bloody slave driver."

Colonel Arbuthnot had lived in an anonymous brick building called Delaware Mansions in a not-so-fashionable part of Kensington that bordered on Notting Hill Gate.

The caretaker was as colorless as the building. She was a

174

thin, gaunt woman with a humorless face, and she was called, aptly, Mrs. Sharpe.

"I don't see that I can let you into the colonel's apartment," she said, sniffing with disapproval.

Sergeant Watkins produced his badge. "North Wales police, Madam. We're investigating the colonel's murder," he said.

That had an instant effect. The woman's eyes almost protruded as if she were a cartoon. "Murder? You're telling me the old colonel has been murdered?" Evan noticed that the upper-class accent had disappeared in favor of good old-fashioned cockney. "Well, well. That's a turn-up for the books. Who'd want to murder him?"

"That's what we're trying to find out," Sergeant Watkins said. "You probably know about his recent doings better than anybody."

"We passed the time of day as he went out," Mrs. Sharpe said, guardedly, in case these policemen were hinting at more than that. "I felt sorry for the old chap. Nobody in the world, that's what he always told me."

"So he had few visitors then?" Evan asked.

"Few? I can't remember any recently. He went out for his walk every morning, around the park, then he stopped to read the papers at the local library and came back in time for lunch. That was about it, really. Not much of a life, was it?"

"He didn't go out apart from that?"

"He had lunch at his club sometimes, although he was telling me that it was hardly worth going there any more because all the old codgers were dead now. And he sometimes went to the pictures in the evenings."

"On his own?"

"Who did he have to go with?" Mrs. Sharpe asked. "I'm sorry to hear he was murdered, but in a way it was a blessing in disguise, wasn't it? He didn't have much to live for."

"Do you think we could take a look at his room now?" Evan asked.

"I can't see what for," Mrs. Sharpe said.

"It might give us some clue about who could have killed him."

"Why, some madman, of course," Mrs. Sharpe said angrily. "Who else would want to kill a harmless old man with no money?"

"All the same, we might find something," Evan insisted. "A letter from a distant relative, his bank book . . ."

"I can tell you that he's had no letters since last Christmas," she said. "I know because I sort the post and put it in their cubbies."

And take a good snoop at it too, Evan thought.

Obviously Watkins was sharing his frustration. "I don't know why you're being so difficult about this, Mrs. Sharpe. I can go to Scotland Yard and come back with a search warrant in fifteen minutes, but then we're only wasting more time, aren't we? So why don't you just cooperate and give us the key to his room—unless you think you've got something to hide in any way?"

That did the trick. "Me?" She drew herself up to her full height and looked down her beaky nose like a bird of prey. "Young man, I have never done anything against the law in my life. Here." She stalked to a glass-fronted cabinet on the wall and almost flung a key at Watkins. "229. At the back on the second floor."

The hallways were unnaturally quiet. The carpet was threadbare and faded. There was an ancient lift with an open, wrought-iron cage, but they took the stairs and passed nobody. The colonel's flat was at the back, facing onto the backs of other buildings, making it dark and dingy. No wonder the colonel had felt so alive when he came to Wales each summer.

The living room was filled with good quality oak furniture—a big rolltop writing desk, a barley twist table and chairs, and an overstuffed leather club chair beside a gas fire. Mementoes of a life spent in the Orient were everywhere—a large bronze Buddha in one corner, a brass-topped coffee table with an oriental water pipe on it, a couple of mogul prints on the walls. On the mantelpiece and on top of the desk were old photos of handsome young men in tropical kit, tiger shoots, Indian palaces, and a large portrait photo of a very beautiful woman. The glass case on the wall was full of silver trophies.

Everything was covered in a layer of dust.

"That's why she didn't want us to see the room," Evan muttered. "She was probably supposed to clean it while he was away and didn't think he'd be back for a while."

Watkins opened the rolltop desk. "Alright," he said. "Let's get down to work. I'll go through the cubbies and the drawers. You look through the kitchen and bedroom for any correspondence or anything else of interest."

The desk was in immaculate order. So were the kitchen and the bedroom. There was a wall calendar of glorious Britain above the fridge, with the weeks in Wales highlighted. The bedside table contained only a book on the history of the Gurkha regiment and a tin of extra strong peppermints. The closet was almost empty. The colonel had taken his meager wardrobe with him.

Evan came back into the living room. "Nothing in there, sarge."

"Not much in here, either. No hidden fortunes turning up. Did you try the mattress?"

"No, but I could. Somehow I don't think the colonel would be stupid enough to put money where old Mrs. Sharp-Eyes could spot it."

"That's probably true enough. I bet she has a good snoop at everything. And she'd love to be part of a murder investigation too. She's the kind that likes to feel important. So if she's got nothing to tell us, then there is nothing to tell."

"Poor old chap," Evan said, taking out an envelope that contained Christmas cards. "Only five Christmas cards and one of those was from an army benevolent association. There don't appear to be any disgruntled relatives waiting in the wings, do there?"

"If there are, they don't keep in touch with him. Look, here's his address book." He flipped through it. Most of the names were crossed out.

"Here's his appointment book," Watkins said, taking out a slim black leather diary. "I don't suppose there's much in it either, but you might take a look."

The diary was almost empty. It confirmed what Mrs. Sharpe had said. The colonel hardly ever went out or entertained. Then an entry, pencilled in tiny, neat script, caught his eye.

"Hey, look at this, sarge," Evan said. "Cynthia, eight P.M. Taffy's. And here it is again in March. And in April. He had a date with this Cynthia once a month."

"A young relative, maybe?"

"She didn't send him a Christmas card."

"It's worth checking out. We'll have to find out where this Taffy's is. Some kind of Welsh restaurant maybe. Something Welsh anyway, with a name like that."

Mrs. Sharpe stuck her head out of her door as they went past. "Find anything interesting?" she asked.

"Did the colonel ever mention anyone called Cynthia?"

"Cynthia? That wasn't his wife's name, was it? No, that was Joanie. He talked about Joanie all the time. I can't say I ever remember Cynthia. He told me they had a daughter who died out in the East long ago."

"No, this person was alive last month," Evan said. "Thanks for your help, Mrs. Sharpe. We might be in touch again, and you can call us if you remember anything at all that might be important."

"Oh, and don't touch anything in the colonel's flat, will you," Sergeant Watkins added. "We might need to take fingerprints, so make sure you don't dust."

He couldn't resist giving Evan a grin as they went out into the street.

"Here's a phone booth," Evan said. "Let's look up this Taffy's. It's a good place to start."

"Not there," Watkins said, a few minutes later. "Either it's not in London or they don't need to advertise. We're coming up against more than our share of dead ends here. I hope this trip doesn't turn out to be a complete waste of time, or I'll have the D.I. yelling that I've used police funds for nothing."

"Not too many police funds, judging by that hotel," Evans said. "I think we should go to Scotland Yard and see what they've got on Ted Morgan."

"Okay with me. Let's get a taxi this time. My feet are already killing me."

Soon they were crawling along Church Street in stop-and-go traffic.

"It would have been quicker to take the tube," Watkins sighed.

"Traffic's bad these days, even at weekends," the cabbie said. "Too many bloody tourists. Where are you gentlemen from?"

"Wales."

"I thought so. I can always spot the accent. Up to see the sights, are you?"

"No, we're police officers on a case," Watkins said.

"Ooh. Police eh? I'm glad I'm not exceeding the speed limit." He laughed at his own joke.

"Tell me," Evan said suddenly. "Do you happen to know a place called Taffy's?"

"Taffy's?" The old cabbie started a chuckle, which turned into the wheez of a smoker's cough. "Then you're planning on taking in a little recreation on the side, are you?"

"You know it then?"

"Of course I know it. Just off Greek Street in Soho."

179

"Could you take us there instead of Scotland Yard?"

"There's no point at this time of day. They don't open until late afternoon."

"Someone might be there. Would you take us, please?"

"Suit yourselves. I'll see if we can nip through the park and get out of this mess."

Fifteen minutes later the taxi came to a halt in a depressing back alley. "Here you are, gents. Taffy's. Enjoy yourselves, eh? But don't do anything I wouldn't do!" He cackled again.

Watkins and Evan climbed out and stood looking around as the taxi drove away. The alley smelled of stale orange peel, rotting garbage, and dog urine. Most of the buildings presented only dirty brick walls and closed doors, but one doorway was open and a flight of stairs led down to a basement. On the open door was a glass-fronted sign. "Taffy's Club. Members Only." On both sides the sign was decorated with pictures of curvaceous girls wearing spiked heels, elaborate feather headdresses, and not much else.

"It's a girlie club! How about that—the old devil." Watkins chuckled. "Put your blinkers on Evans, we're going in!"

Evan followed him down the stairs through swing doors into a vestibule with red satin walls and sofas and a red plush carpet. On the wall were framed prints of Botticelli nudes. There were several doors, all closed. While they were deciding which door to try first they heard the clatter of high heels coming down the stairs and a girl burst in. She wasn't wearing makeup, hair curlers were peeping out from under a scarf, and she had dark circles under her eyes. It was hard to equate her with one of the beauties on the poster above. She reacted like a startled fawn when she saw them.

" 'Ere, what are you doing 'ere?" she demanded. "We ain't open. Go on, clear off before Barry sees yer. Come back at four o'clock. That's when we open."

"We've come to see the boss," Watkins said. "Tell him we're here, will you?"

"The boss? Barry, you mean?"

"Is he the owner?"

"No, he's just the manager."

"Where's the owner then?"

"I don't know. I just work here, don't I?" she demanded. "What do you want to know for anyway?"

"Just a little social call from back home," Watkins said. "Taffy's is a Welsh name, isn't it, and as you can hear, we're from Wales."

"The owner wouldn't be from Wales by any chance, would he?" Evan asked.

"I wouldn't know. Like I said, I just—"

"Work here. We know," Watkins finished for her.

At that moment the door on the far left opened and a young dark haired man came out. He had sharp dark eyes, a very short haircut, combed forward like one of the old Romans, and he was wearing an expensive dark suit.

"Noreen, you're late," he barked. Then he noticed Watkins and Evans. "We're closed."

"So this young lady told us," Watkins said. "Are you Barry?"

"What if I am?"

"We'd like a word. North Wales police." He flashed the ID.

"I'm busy. What's it about?"

"Do you have an office we can go to?" Evan asked.

"We can talk here just as well. I'm not supposed to take people back to the office."

"Why? Got anything to hide back there?" Watkins asked with a sweet smile.

"Just obeying orders," Barry said.

"Okay, Barry. Let's sit down here," Watkins said, choosing the closer of the two red sofas. "We'd like to speak to the owner. Where can we find him?"

"He's away at the moment."

"Away? You mean out of the country?"

"Could be. I'm not sure. He don't confide in me. I just work here."

"When will he be back?" Evan asked.

"I couldn't say."

"Alright. You've got a girl who works here called Cynthia?"

"That's right. One of our best little workers." Barry attempted a smile.

"Can we talk to her?"

"She ain't here yet."

"Then give us her home address."

"She's asleep right now. She needs her beauty sleep, you know. You'll have to come back later, won't yer. She gets in around three."

Watkins sighed impatiently. "Okay. Then do you remember a customer called Colonel Arbuthnot?"

"Never heard of him."

"We know he came here on a regular basis, so he'd have to be a member, wouldn't he?"

"It's possible. Many of the gentlemen give fictitious names, don't they? They don't want the little woman to find out where they've been." Barry gave them a supercilious smile.

"Then let's check your records."

Barry stood up. "If you want to check anything here, you'd better bloody well come back with a search warrant," he said.

"No problem. We'll do that," Sergeant Watkins said. "And don't go trying to hide things either, because we'll keep searching until we find what we want."

"What exactly do you want?"

"To find out who had reason to bash an old bloke over the head," Evans said, and was pleased to see the startled reaction on Barry's face.

Chapter 19

"There's something fishy going on at that place," Watkins muttered to Evan as they took a cab to New Scotland Yard. "I just hope he doesn't manage to hide too much evidence before we get back."

"It's not our problem anyway, is it?" Evans asked. "It's up to the local vice squad if they're doing anything illegal there. We just need to know if the colonel could be in any way mixed up in it."

"Like what?"

"Extortion? Blackmail?"

"But you don't kill off the one who's paying out."

"Unless he refuses to pay."

"Possible. More likely than someone in Llanfair wanting to get rid of him."

"He may have threatened to go to the police with something he knew about Taffy's Club," Evan pointed out.

"I don't see how he could do that without incriminating himself."

"You know the colonel—he was one of the old school. If he found something wrong, he'd feel it was his job to report it, at whatever personal cost."

The taxi pulled up outside the new concrete and glass building that housed the headquarters of the Metropolitan Police.

Evan peered up at the building as he got out of the cab. "Doesn't it seem odd to you that nobody at Taffy's seemed to know anything about the owner—where he was, who he was?"

"I expect they were just being cagey," Watkins replied as they headed for the revolving glass doors.

The young female P.C. at the front desk explained that being Saturday, there weren't too many people on duty. "What branch did you want?" she asked.

"Let's start with vice," Watkins said. "They'd know about Taffy's if there is anything worth knowing."

She glanced at her computer. "I've got Sergeant Dobson in. I'll give him a call and let him know you're here."

A few minutes later they were sitting in a cramped back office, divided from its fellows by glass partitions. The view was of more brick walls with a small slice of River Thames between them. The desk was piled high with papers and a worried-looking plainclothes officer looked up from a computer as they came in. "Sorry about the mess," he said. "I still can't trust my notes to computers. I have to keep a printout of everything."

"I feel the same way," Watkins said. He held out his hand. "Sergeant Watkins and Constable Evans, North Wales police."

"Jim Dobson. Take a pew if you can find anywhere to sit." Sergeant Dobson snatched up a pile of papers and added them to the tottering mound on the desk. "Now, what can I do for you?"

"What can you tell us about a club called Taffy's?" Watkins asked.

A smile crossed Jim Dobson's face. "Taffy's? I could tell you more than you probably want to hear. What do you want to know about it?"

"Anything you can tell us. Who owns it?" Evan said.

"It's owned by a bloke called Taffy Jones. He's got fingers

in all sorts of nasty little pies—escort services, clip joints, prostitution, drugs. You name it, he's into it."

"Taffy Jones—is he a Welshman then?"

"Originally, I suppose. You wouldn't think so from talking to him."

"Any idea where we'd find him?"

"I'd like to know that myself. So would half of London, I'd imagine. It seems that Mr. Taffy Jones has done a bunk, leaving a lot of people not very happy, including a rather large protection racket, to whom he owes a great deal of money."

"This Taffy Jones," Evan asked. "What does he look like?"

"Good-looking sort of bloke, big, solidly built—a bit like you." He nodded at Evan. "Late thirties, early forties. Snappy dresser."

"I think we might know where he is," Evan said.

"We might?" Watkins turned to him.

"In the police morgue in Bangor," Evan said.

"Ted Morgan, you mean?" Sergeant Watkins demanded.

Evan nodded. "It all ties in, doesn't it? Arriving like that out of the blue, bringing nothing with him but clothes. He was hiding out."

Watkins turned to Jim Dobson. "Any idea whether Taffy Jones could have been an alias?"

"No idea at all. Taffy Jones is the only name we've known him by here. You say he's dead?"

"If it's the same man, someone put a bullet in his head. Maybe the protection racketeers caught up with him."

"Is that a fact?" Jim Dobson took out a cigarette. "Smoke?" He offered the packet. "Mind if I do? Filthy habit but I don't have time to quit."

He lit the cigarette and drew deeply on it. "Put a bullet in his head, you say? Execution style?"

"Not really. A neat little bullet between the eyes from a small revolver."

Dobson shook his head. "That doesn't sound like their

185

style at all. A burst of machine gun fire from a passing car or torching his house would be more like it. Or if they got hold of him, one bullet to the back of the head with his arms bound behind his back. Of course, I'm sure Mr. Jones had many enemies outside of any protection racket. He always liked to sail close to the wind, but he was a sharp one. I have to say that for him. We never managed to shut him down. God knows we tried enough, but he was always one step ahead of us."

"Somebody has managed to shut him down now," Evan said, "if he turns out to be the same person."

"Have you got a photo?"

"Only with a hole in his head," Watkins said and produced it. "But I think you could still identify him from that."

Dobson studied it. "Looks pretty much like him," he said. "So how did you manage to connect him with Taffy's club?"

"Pure luck," Evan said. "We were looking into another murder that took place last week. An old colonel on holiday had his head bashed in. It turned out he was a regular visitor to Taffy's." He looked up with an excited smile on his face. "And I think we might have found out who killed him!"

"We have? Who?" Watkins asked.

"Look, sarge. How does this sound? The colonel recognized someone in the village and was surprised to see them there. He was telling me about it at the pub and then he suddenly shut up and made up a ridiculous story. Ted Morgan, Taffy Jones, that is, was at the pub that night. If he was hiding out in Llanfair, he wouldn't want to be recognized, would he? He thought he was safe up there. Everyone knew him as Ted Morgan, and how many outsiders come to a little village like Llanfair? It was just bad luck that the colonel was there. He couldn't risk the colonel going back to London and blabbing that he'd seen him, so he crept out of the pub behind him, bashed him over the head, and came back to join the group."

186

"But wouldn't you have noticed him going out after the colonel?" Watkins asked.

"It's possible he could have sneaked out with all the excitement that was going on that night. I never thought of that before. He might have gone to the bathroom, then dashed out through the back entrance, killed the old man, and come back in the same way. It was risky, but there's a chance that nobody missed him for a short while."

"You might have something there," Watkins agreed.

"It has to be right, sarge. He was probably scared silly that the colonel would go back to London and announce to all and sundry that he'd seen Taffy Jones calling himself by another name in Llanfair. He couldn't take that risk."

"Okay, but the colonel didn't get a chance to talk to anybody, did he?" Watkins said. "So who else knew that Ted Morgan was Taffy Jones?"

"Someone else in London must have known where he had gone," Watkins suggested.

Dobson shook his head. "Nobody we've talked to, and I can tell you the underworld types are very anxious to find him. Of course, they'd like to get to him first. Did he have any close friends or relatives in the village who might have known the truth about him?"

Evan shook his head. "Only his sister, and he wasn't on speaking terms with her. He hadn't been near the place for twenty years. Everyone thought he was a successful London businessman."

"He was, in a way," Dobson commented dryly. "Just not in the way they thought."

Evan smiled grimly. "The only address we had for him was a posh place in Mayfair that turned out to be a mail drop. That's where his father had always written to."

"Someone recognized him," Dobson said. "Someone who had a score to settle with him."

"We should go back and take a look at the club," Watkins said. "They must keep a list of members. Maybe a name will show up or maybe he's got some personal correspondence tucked away. Was he married?"

"Divorced," Dobson said. "And don't look for the ex wife as a likely suspect. He was paying her off very nicely, so we hear. He had to buy her silence, didn't he?"

He got to his feet. "Do you want me to come down to the club with you? They know me there and they won't give me the runaround."

"This character called Barry said we'd need a search warrant," Watkins said cautiously.

"Search warrant. Barry Oates knows where I'd shove a search warrant. He knows I've got enough on him to put him away for life if he so much as breathes at the wrong time."

"Thanks," Watkins said. "We'll need all the help we can get if we're going to get to the bottom of this thing." They followed Jim Dobson through the deserted corridors of New Scotland Yard and down a back elevator to the garage.

"I told you we'd be back, didn't I?" Sergeant Watkins gave Barry Oates a triumphant smile as they swept through the swing doors into Taffy's again. "Brought a friend to see you too."

"Hello, Barry. Is business booming without the boss around to keep an eye on you?" Dobson asked pleasantly. "Heard from him lately, have you? No postcard from Rio or Buenos Aires?"

"Get stuffed, Dobson," Barry said. "What do you want, anyway?"

"Just a friendly visit, Barry. I wanted to show these two friends of mine the inner sanctum—the boss's office. So open up."

"I don't know what you think you're going to find. We've got nothing to hide. See for yourself." He pushed past Jim

Dobson, led them down a narrow hallway, and opened a door leading into the room beyond. It was tastefully decorated with a large oak desk, thick pile carpet, and subdued lighting. It could have been the office of any executive.

"Be my guest," Barry said and sat in the leather armchair in one corner.

A search of the desk produced a revolving file of names, including the colonel's. But no other name that they recognized.

"There are no account books here," Watkins commented.

"Yeah, well, this is a classy joint. We 'ave an accountant do the books, don't we?" Barry said. "I can give you his name. 'E'll be in on Monday. But you won't find nothing there you can stick on us."

"I think we're wasting our time," Watkins muttered to Evans. "If there was anything here, it's been whisked away."

"I don't even know what there could have been," Evan said. "You don't keep copies of blackmail notes or threatening letters, do you?"

"Who said anything about blackmail?" Barry demanded. "We're not involved in nothin' sordid like that. Just good clean fun here. Ask the sergeant." He grinned at Dobson.

"We'll get you one day, Barry. No rush," Dobson said easily. "Now, if you could just help us find your boss, we'd all be a lot happier, wouldn't we? Any idea if he might have been going to Wales, for example?"

Barry's look of genuine surprise was apparent for a second before he regained his composure. "You mean he might have gone to visit the old folks back home? Well, isn't that nice?"

His eyes went to a picture on the wall. It was of Snowdon from Llyn Llydaw. The trees were in full fall colors and the lake reflected the peak above. Evan went over to look at it. A photo album was lying on top of the credenza—an impressive-looking book with a tooled leather cover. Evan wondered if it contained more photos of Wales. Maybe Ted Morgan had secretly longed for his birthplace after all.

189

He opened the book and almost closed it again. It wasn't Welsh mountains at all, but scantily clad girls in provocative poses. Watkins came over to join him.

"Samples to show the clients?" he asked Barry.

"Seen one you fancy?" Barry asked insolently. "I could set you up for later today. For a nice supper together, I mean. Or a game of darts?"

"I don't think the wife would like it, somehow," Watkins said. He went on turning pages. "Miss Cynthia Cardew. She'll show you the sportin' life," he read, pointing at a photo of an aristocratic-looking young woman wearing a riding cap and not much else and holding a riding crop in her hand. "I must say the Colonel had good taste. I'd still like to talk to her." He turned the page again. "Phew. It's warm in here, isn't it?" He tugged at his collar and nudged Evan good-naturedly. "You shouldn't be looking at this stuff, young kid of your age." He went to close the book. Evan stopped him.

"Here, hold on a minute, sarge. Turn back to that last page."

"See one you like?" Sergeant Watkins chuckled.

The page fell open. The girl had one high heeled foot on a bearskin rug and a big ostrich feather fan covered part of her naked body as she peeked provocatively around it. Evan stared at the picture in disbelief. Even with the tumble of platinum blond curls and the Marilyn Monroe makeup he could recognize her. The caption underneath read, "Anita Dove. She'll take you to new flights of fancy."

"Look, sarge." Evan pointed fiercely at the photo. "It's Annie Pigeon!"

Chapter 19

"Give me a chance to talk to her first, sarge," Evan suggested as the train pulled into Bangor station. It was past eight o'clock but still light, although the sun was hidden behind ominous clouds. The ocean was slate gray and flecked with whitecaps.

"Home sweet home," Watkins said.

They had rushed straight from Taffy's to take the next train home. A phone call to D.I. Hughes had revealed that he was away fishing for the weekend at an unknown destination and couldn't be reached until Monday. Now they were both tired and on edge.

"I think we should bring her in for questioning," Sergeant Watkins said, getting his bag down from the rack as the train came to a halt. "I don't see any reason for letting you meet with her first. You'd probably be softhearted enough to help her talk her way out of this."

"Not this time," Evan said firmly. "I don't like being made a fool of, sarge, and she made a bloody fool of me. She saw me as a good-natured, helpful chump who also happened to be a policeman, and she used me." He thumped his fist against his open palm. "She really had me fooled. That act of polite indifference when we met Ted Morgan up on the hill—as if she didn't know him from Adam. And all that panic about a prowler—it was just a setup so that she could claim her gun had been stolen. She showed up the moment she heard that we had ruled out suicide. She knew that we'd find her prints on it."

Watkins opened the door and stepped down onto the platform. "But you said she seemed genuinely scared. Do you think she lured you round to her place and kept you there while a boyfriend lurking outside did the actual killing?"

"No." Evan shook his head angrily. "I've been doing a lot of thinking on the train, and I think she lured me to her house so that she'd have the perfect alibi while she did the killing herself."

They joined a jostling crowd of arriving tourists and dodged past suitcases, strollers, and little kids.

"How did she manage that?" Watkins muttered.

"She got me to read a bedtime story to her child. I wondered at the time why she insisted on this particular story. She said it was the kid's favorite, but it wasn't. Now I know why— it was the longest one she could find. It must have taken me fifteen minutes to get through it and then, of course, the little girl wanted another one. All that time Annie was out of the room, supposedly downstairs opening a bottle of wine, leaving the girl and me alone to get to know each other better. That's what she said. She would have had plenty of time to get to Ted Morgan's bungalow, shoot him, and come back. No wonder her hand was shaking when she poured that wine!"

"But what about the colonel?" Watkins asked as they reached his car in the parking lot. "She couldn't have killed him, could she?"

"I'm not so sure about that now," Evan said. He was remembering the colonel blundering out of the pub in a panic, almost colliding with Annie who had just come in. "She could have been the person he recognized, not Ted Morgan, who was still in the lounge with his old cronies."

"What motive could she have had?"

"The same as Ted Morgan, I'd imagine. What if she came here deliberately to kill Ted, sure that nobody would know her here or link her to him. Then she sees the colonel, who recognizes her as a girl from Taffy's club. Now she'll be tied to Ted's death if the colonel blabs. He has to go. She left the pub right after him too."

He climbed into the car beside Watkins, who said. "And you think she'd be more likely to confess to you?"

"It's possible," Evan said. "At least I'd like to find out why she did it."

"She's a cool customer and she wanted Ted Morgan out of the way. What's the betting he's the father of her kid? Maybe he had life insurance money settled on the child. Who knows?"

"Will you let me talk to her in her own home? Whatever Annie's really like, Jenny is a sweet little kid and I'd hate her to be scared by having her mother hauled away in the middle of the night."

Watkins sighed. "Alright. Go ahead and talk to her, but I'm putting a couple of men to watch her house. I don't want to risk her doing a bunk during the night. And you might want to watch yourself too. If she's killed twice, there's nothing to stop her from killing again. We don't know that was her only gun, do we?"

"I'll be careful," Evans said. "I'd like to think that I can persuade her to give herself up."

"Just make sure she doesn't persuade you to let her slip out through the back window," Watkins said dryly. "Whatever happens, I'm bringing her in first thing tomorrow. Make sure she knows that."

The cottage door opened a crack in response to the knock. Annie Pigeon's suspicious face peered around it. A smile of disbelief spread across her face and she threw the door open wide.

"I couldn't think who it could be, calling so late at night. Excuse the robe. I've just had a bath." She was still smiling up at him, her eyes flirting. "I didn't expect to see you—I heard you'd gone away for the weekend."

"That's right," Evans said. "I decided to come home early."

"What was it, business or recreation?"

"A bit of both," Evan said. "I decided to go for recreation to a place that had been recommended to me."

"Oh, what was that?" She was still relaxed, smiling up at him with innocent blue eyes. She was dressed in a fluffy white bathrobe and Evan found it hard to believe that he was confronting a killer.

"A place called Taffy's Club. Only it seemed that the young lady I requested wasn't available any longer. Pity really, her picture was still in the album."

"You'd better come in," she said. She glanced up and down the street. "Here, what's going on?" she asked, her voice sharp now.

"You tell me," Evan said. "That's right. It *is* a police car parked over there. Your house is being watched, so don't get any funny ideas."

She touched his sleeve. "Evan, I can explain everything."

"It better be good," Evan said. He shepherded her into the living room and waited until she sat in the vinyl armchair. He perched on a fold-up chair in the corner.

"How did you ever find out?" she asked. Her face, without its usual mask of makeup, matched the whiteness of the fluffy robe.

"You must have thought I was very stupid," Evan said, trying to control the anger in his voice. "I bet you couldn't believe your luck when I rescued your daughter and you realized you'd got a tame village bobby who probably wasn't too bright. You certainly worked hard enough on it, didn't you—asking me to show you around, feeding me all that rubbish about how fond of me your daughter was so that I'd be fooled into reading her a bedtime story. I can understand now that you were setting me up, but using your daughter—"

"That part was true," she said. "She thought you were the nicest man she'd ever met. She did talk about you all the time."

"That was a lucky break for you, wasn't it then? You had me trapped here—your perfect alibi while you went and killed Ted Morgan."

"I didn't kill Ted Morgan!" she exclaimed.

"Oh no? Where did you go then? A late-night stroll around the village with your gun in your hand?"

"You have to believe me, Evan. I swear it."

"It's not me you have to convince—it's the jury. And quite frankly I think you're going to have a hard time convincing them that you're innocent when your prints are on the gun, you lured me here to give you an alibi, and you worked for Ted Morgan as a call girl. They'll probably get you on two counts of murder in fact—"

"Two counts?"

"The colonel. He was a regular customer at the club. You recognized each other, didn't you? You were scared he'd give you away. He was bound to put two and two together when you killed Ted, so he had to go. You left the pub right after he did. And you knew he was murdered when everyone else still thought it was an accident."

"I saw Ted slinking back from the direction of the river," she said flatly. "I thought I recognized the old bloke from the club in London, so I figured it out."

"But you didn't say anything to the police about it."

"Do you think I was stupid? Ted Morgan wasn't the kind of man you take chances with."

"So you killed him."

"I swear to you I didn't. I wished him dead, but I didn't kill him."

"Then how come it was your gun, your bullet? There

195

wasn't ever a prowler or a break-in, was there. If someone had broken into your house, a gun would be the first thing you'd check on. You only discovered it was missing when we ruled out suicide and it looked as if you might be suspect number one."

She slumped back into the chair, looking very small and frightened. "Okay, so I went to his house that night, but I didn't kill him."

"But you took the gun with you?"

"I wanted to frighten him."

"To do what?"

"To leave me and Jenny alone." She closed her eyes and sighed. "I really thought I'd managed to get away this time. I thought we'd be alright here and we could have a good life."

"Don't give me that," Evan snapped. "You came here to kill Ted Morgan. You probably thought you'd get away with it because nobody would suspect you knew each other. What did you do—arrange a rendezvous to lure him here? I couldn't get over how polite you were to each other when we met on the hill."

"I didn't know he was going to be here." Her voice was almost a hysterical sob by now. "I got the shock of my life when we bumped into him on that hill. I had no idea—"

"Oh come on, Annie. You expect me to believe that?"

"I swear I didn't know he was here. I knew he was Welsh and that was all. I had no idea he'd even left London. Then to get here and see him—I didn't know what to do. I suppose I panicked."

"And shot him."

"No." She gave a tired sigh and closed her eyes. "You probably can't imagine what it was like and what it felt like to get away." She sat up again. "I suppose I should start at the beginning. My mum died when I was a little kid. My father married again and my new stepmum didn't want me around the house. She kicked me out when I was sixteen. I'd been taking dance lessons when my mum was alive and I had this dream of becoming a dancer. So I went up to London to get into a West End show. Of course, it wasn't that easy, was it.

"Anyway, I met this girl, Glynis, at an audition. She'd run away from home and she was having a hard time too. So we got a room together and pooled money to buy food. Then she came home all excited one day and said she'd met this man from back home and he might hire us as dancers in this West End nightclub. Well, we were all excited. We'd been living on baked beans for a month and we didn't have the rent. So we went to meet him and he was a real smoothy. He told us that we'd have to start out as hostesses and he'd move us up to dancers when he thought we were ready. He gave us stage names. I was Anita Dove, Glyn was Desirée St. Claire. Pretty fancy, eh?"

She closed her eyes again and sighed. "Of course, hostesses really meant prostitutes. We only found out that too late. I was still a virgin. So was Glynis. Taffy—Ted Morgan, that is—came into my room and raped me. When I cried afterward he said, 'One day you're going to get to like this. You won't be able to get enough of it.' Then he gave me something to make me feel better. It was coke. He liked to have all his hookers hooked, so to speak. That way you were dependent on him.

"Poor old Glyn. She really did get hooked on the stuff. She was in a bad way. She just couldn't handle what we were doing. 'If my dad could see me now,' she said. She killed herself. Took an overdose. I found her. Poor kid—she was so homesick. She used to talk about Wales all the time and show me pictures. Remember that picture on Ted's office wall? It used to make her cry. 'That's my home,' she'd say. 'That's where I belong.' "

"And what about you?" Evan asked quietly.

"Me? I kept on going. I was really doing quite well, rising through the profession, so to speak." She gave a twisted smile. "If you worked well, Taffy was nice to you. If you did something wrong, watch out. The one thing he didn't let you do was leave. Girls who left had a habit of winding up dead."

"But you left?"

"I had to, didn't I? I always was the stupid one. After Glynis died I got really depressed and I went on this blinder—booze, coke, the lot. I was passed out all weekend. Of course, that meant I didn't take my pill for three days. So guess who gets pregnant. Taffy was furious. He sent me to get an abortion. But I couldn't go through with it. I mean, poor little kid, it wasn't her fault, was it? So I climbed out through the back window of the clinic and ran away. I went as far away as I could and I wound up at a shelter in Manchester. They were nice to me there. They took care of me while I had the baby, then they found me a cheap place to live while I was on the dole. But it was a bad part of town and I was scared of how Jenny would grow up. The kids she started playing with—they were teaching her bad words and all that stuff."

She looked down at her hands then slowly raised her eyes to meet Evan's. "That's when I decided to come here. It was Glynis' paradise. Maybe it would be paradise for me too." She paused and took a deep breath. "And then *he* showed up. I nearly died. I thought, There's nowhere to run any more. I've got to stand and fight. So I went over there with the gun. I told him if he didn't leave me and Jenny alone, I'd kill him. He just laughed and he took the gun away from me. He had that sort of power. I don't know who killed him, but I'm glad he's dead."

She got up and walked over to the window, pulled the curtain back, then let it fall again. "You're right. The jury will never believe me, will they?"

She paced around the room like a trapped animal. Then she stopped. "Look, Evan. I'm sorry I got you into this. I'm sorry I set you up. But it's true what I said about Jenny. She said you were the kindest man she ever met. I think so too."

Evan sat perched on the edge of the chair, fighting conflicting emotions. He wanted to get up, put his arms around her, and tell her that it was going to be alright. But he couldn't. She had fooled him once before. How was he to know she wasn't fooling him with a sob story this time?

"Is there anyone who could back up your story?"

"Not that Ted Morgan was alive and laughing when I left him," she said bitterly. "And probably nobody would be willing to talk about what went on in London. They're all too scared. Even though he's dead now, they'd probably worry that someone would get them. Glynis would have told you. Me and Glyn—we would have done anything for each other."

She reached down to the bookcase and picked up a photograph album. "This is the only photo of her I've got," she said. "We went to Kew Gardens on one of those riverboats when we first met. We couldn't really afford it, but it was such a beautiful day. We took a picnic. It was one of the best days of my life."

She opened the book and pointed to a snapshot. Two girls were standing under a lilac tree in full bloom. They looked young and carefree, like schoolgirls on a class outing. Annie's fair curls contrasted with Glynis' long dark hair. Underneath she had printed, in girlish letters. "Me and Glynis Dawson. May 3rd, 1993."

"One of the gardeners took it for us," she said.

Evan got to his feet. "Dawson? Glynis Dawson, you say? And she came from around here?"

"Yes. Not from Llanfair, but down the pass at a place called Beddgelert. I'd like to have moved there, but it's more expensive and upscale, isn't it? Hey, what's the matter? Where are you going?"

He was already halfway to the front door.

"Don't go anywhere. I'll be back," he yelled, slamming the door behind him.

Chapter 20

Night had fallen and the storm which had threatened earlier was now blowing in full force as Evan drove down the pass toward Beddgelert. Rain lashed against the windscreen and great gusts of wind buffeted the small car so that Evan had to fight to keep it on the narrow road. He was well aware that beyond that low wall there was a long sheer drop to the lake below. He tried to turn up the wipers but they were already going at full speed, unable to cope with the amount of water that streamed down the glass. The headlights cut a pitifully small arc of light into the blackness of the Nantgwynant Pass. Each hairpin curve appeared with alarming suddenness and each time Evan had the impression of swinging into nothing.

I should have called Watkins, Evan thought. He realized now that he had acted impulsively, rushing out alone into the dark. Wasn't it a basic premise of police training that you went out in twos whenever possible? He had been so excited when the pieces finally fell into place. He was sure his hunch had to be right. He just prayed it was. He didn't want Annie Pigeon to spend the rest of her life in jail.

Lights of Beddgelert appeared through the curtain of rain,

and he was driving past neat gray stone houses. He crossed the bridge and swung into the courtyard of the Royal Stag Hotel. Lights were shining from every room and it looked solid and welcoming—a tall, gray stone building with the white stag sign swinging in the wind outside.

Evan found a parking spot between a Mercedes and a Jag. Obviously it wasn't cheap to stay at the Royal Stag. The reception desk was unoccupied, but voices were coming from the bar on his left. He pushed open the door and found himself in what must be a foreigner's fantasy of a British pub. The walls were old oak panelling. Heavy oak beams spanned the ceiling, decorated with horse brasses. Horse brasses adorned the pillars of the bar too. In the middle of one wall a roaring fire crackled in a massive brick fireplace, even though it was summer. At the far end of the room a group was assembled around a piano, laughing as they tried out various show tunes.

Mr. Dawson was standing at the bar, deep in conversation with a customer. He was relaxed and smiling, dressed in twill slacks, a lamb's wool cardigan over an open necked checked shirt—very different from the scarlet faced, shouting man Evan had seen before.

"So I told the golf pro," he was saying as Evan approached discreetly, "what he could do with his bloody club."

His audience laughed. Mr. Dawson looked up to see Evan standing there.

"Are you looking for someone?" he asked.

"You're Mr. Dawson, aren't you?" Evan asked. "I'd like a word if you can spare a minute."

He motioned Evan toward the empty reception area then followed him. "A word about what? Do I know you?"

"P.C. Evans. Llanfair police, sir," Evan said. "And the word's about a man called Ted Morgan."

"Ted Morgan? Never heard of him."

"And a young girl called Desiree St. Claire."

The color drained from Dawson's face. "We can't talk

here," he muttered, looking around. "Hold on a minute while I get a jacket. It's raining, isn't it?"

"Pouring."

"I'll just tell Howard to keep an eye on things until I get back," he said. He disappeared into a back room, then came out again, already halfway into a waterproof jacket. "Let's go," he said. He led Evan to a hunter green Jaguar parked in the slot marked Owner.

"Get in," he said. "I don't want anybody spying on us. News travels quickly in a place like this. I don't want anyone to think that the hotel's having trouble with the law."

Evan hesitated as he opened the passenger door, then got in. The car took off with a great surge of power, roaring through the deserted streets until the village was left behind.

"Okay, what have you got to say to me?" he asked Evan.

"I think you know that, sir," Evan said. "I was in London, at a place called Taffy's Club. I talked to a girl who had worked there with your daughter. I wanted to say that I can understand why you killed Ted Morgan. I might have done the same if it had been my daughter."

Mr. Dawson gave a short, bitter laugh. "Yes, but it won't make any difference in court, will it? It will still be jail for life."

"I'm sure the sentence would be a light one, considering the emotional distress you've gone through."

"But prison, just the same." He sighed as he continued to swing the big car around the hairpin bends. "I'll tell you right now that I'm not sorry. He was a monster. He took away everything I ever loved. He deserved to die. I hope he rots in hell."

"Maybe he did deserve to die," Evan said, "but it wasn't up to you to pass judgement, was it?"

Dawson drove on, tight-lipped as the tires screeched on the bends. "I didn't give you chaps enough credit," he said at last. "I was sure I could pass it off as a suicide. I couldn't believe it when I saw him at that meeting, smiling, jovial, acting like the local benefactor—after what he did to my daughter. Ted Morgan, you say his real name was?"

Evan nodded.

Mr. Dawson took a deep, drawn out breath that sounded like a sigh. "I saw him in London, after the inquest. I went round to Taffy's club to see for myself what hell she'd been through. That Ted Morgan character was playing the genial host. He'd already got another girl to take my Glynis's place." His voice cracked and he was silent for a moment and the only sounds were the deep growl of the engine and rushing of the wind.

"I wanted to kill him then, of course. I could have killed him then, if I'd had a chance. But I didn't have a weapon on me. I'd like to have throttled him with my bare hands but I couldn't get near him with all those bodyguards. I never thought I'd see him again and then there he was, playing public benefactor. I couldn't believe my luck." He chuckled as he swung the wheel around and the tires responded, screeching. "I went round to see him after the meeting. He didn't know who I was, of course. I told him I was interested in investing in his new scheme and he invited me in. Even offered me a drink. He sat there, calm and relaxed, telling me his plans. He looked up and I shot him. Right between the eyes. I always was a good shot. I do a lot of hunting in the winter."

Evan was very aware that they had been climbing steadily back up the pass, the way he had come.

"So your men figured it out, did they? I suppose your D.I.—Hughes, isn't it—had a whole team brainstorming on the case. Did you get Scotland Yard in on it too?"

"No, it was sheer luck, actually," Evan said. "Sheer bad luck for you, Mr. Dawson. I was shown a picture of Glynis and I found out that her last name was Dawson. That rang a bell because my landlady had told me all about you when you ran out of the meeting. I put two and two together and came straight to you."

"Then I'd say it was your bad luck," Mr. Dawson said. He swung into a small parking lot at the scenic overlook and brought the car to a screeching halt. "Get out, please."

"Don't do anything stupid." Evan fought to keep his voice calm. "It will only make things worse."

"For whom? Not for me," Dawson said, and he laughed. "Nobody knows you're here except you and me. Go on, get out."

"What are you going to do—try and make a break for it? How far do you think you could drive before they get you?"

"Oh, I'm not going anywhere," Dawson said. "You are. You are going to have an unfortunate fall. Heaven knows what you were doing up here in the dark, but you missed your footing and plummeted down onto those rocks."

"Do you think you're strong enough to throw me over the edge?" Evan asked.

"Oh no, I know I'm not strong enough to throw you over," Dawson said, and drew out a revolver. "Go on, get out."

Evan opened the car door and stepped out into the storm. He tried to think clearly what would be his best course of action. It was pitch dark. Maybe if he dropped over the parapet he could get away among the rocks, but maybe not. He didn't know if Dawson had a flashlight in the car. If he tried to run for it, he'd be shot in the back. As the man had said, he was a very good shot. He'd got Ted Morgan clean between the eyes. The only question now was whether Dawson would shoot him in cold blood.

Dawson got out after him, the revolver levelled at Evan's head all the time. "Over to the edge," he said, motioning with a jerk of his head.

"Don't you think they'll be suspicious when they find a bullet wound? You think they can't trace guns? And someone's bound to see the car."

"Who? Not too many cars around on a night like this, are

204

there? And there won't be a bullet hole. Like I said, I'm a good shot—I'll just wing you, enough to make you lose your balance and fall."

"You won't get away with this," Evan yelled above the wind. He prayed for a car to come up the pass, but inky blackness surrounded them. It was late for Wales. Everybody would be safely home by now, especially on a night like this.

"I don't see why not," Dawson yelled back. "They've no way of linking me to the killing. After that meeting I drove straight home. I made sure I was seen in the bar before I slipped out of the fire exit and came back. And they won't find my fingerprints anywhere either. I used Ted Morgan's own gun and wiped off my prints before I put it in his hand." He laughed again and Evan saw now that this was a man who had finally cracked under the weight of his despair. He knew that Mr. Dawson wouldn't hesitate to shoot him.

"That was a bit of luck, wasn't it?" he said, coming closer to Evan and making Evan take a step back toward the low wall above the drop. "I couldn't believe it. I had my own gun in my pocket, but his was right there on the table, within my reach— a real gift, don't you think? That's when I was sure I could make it look like suicide."

"But you couldn't, could you?" Evan demanded. Almost horizontal rain was stinging his face and his teeth were chattering from cold and shock. "And it wasn't Ted Morgan's gun either."

Mr. Dawson hesitated. "It wasn't?"

"It belonged to a girl called Annie Pigeon. Ted Morgan took it away from her. The police think she killed him. In fact they have her under surveillance at this moment. The gun's got her prints on it and I expect they'll find her prints in Morgan's living room. Do you know who Annie Pigeon was? Does the name ring a bell? She was Glynis' best friend at the club in London."

"Annie?" The gun wavered. "She wrote about Annie in her suicide note. She said she was sorry she had to leave Annie alone with them."

"Well, Annie's not alone any more," Evan said. "She's got a child and she probably can't even guess who the father is. You can imagine what she's been through, can't you? Do you want her to go to jail for you now? And what about the little girl? What's going to happen to her?"

He saw a spasm of pain cross Dawson's face.

"Do you really think you'll find peace if you kill me?"

"No," Dawson said. "I'll never find peace, not as long as I live. I've been living in hell, ever since she ran away. It was all my fault, you see. I was too strict on her. She was so precious to me, I worried something would happen to her so I wouldn't let her out. I drove her to that life and that end."

"Then give another girl like her a chance," Evan pleaded. "Don't let Annie Pigeon go to jail for a murder she didn't commit."

Dawson's face quivered, then he shook his head violently. "Damn you," he said. He threw down the gun and ran back to the car. The engine was still idling. Evans wasn't sure whether Dawson intended to run him down. The big car seemed to come right at him. He flung himself aside, slipped on the wet gravel and staggered into the wall as the car passed him, inches away. He scrambled to his feet and started to run after it in a futile chase back down to the valley. Dawson was driving absurdly fast. He came to the first hairpin and didn't even bother to swing the wheel around. The car mounted the low wall, was airborne for a moment. Lights cut a crazy arc in the black emptiness. Then there was a sickening crash of glass and metal, followed by an explosion. A ball of flame shot into the air. Then silence.

206

Chapter 21

Bronwen opened her front door to put out her milk bottles. The storm had passed over and stars shone from a clear sky. Above Glyder Fawr the moon was rising, bathing the peaks in a cold light. The air smelled fresh and green and Bronwen stood in the doorway, breathing deeply. She was about to shut the door again when she saw a dark figure running down the road from the pass. Curiosity prevented her from closing the door again. A late-night jogger? Surely not on a night like this.

Then a cracked voice called out, "Bron? Is that you?"

She ran down the path to her front gate. "Evan? What are you doing here? They said you'd gone away for the weekend."

"I came back early," he said. She started as she got her first good look at him in the light. His hair was plastered to his forehead and blood was running down his cheek from an ugly-looking wound. His clothes were covered with mud.

"What on earth have you been doing to yourself?" she asked in horror. "You're soaked to the skin. And you're bleeding."

"I'm alright," he said, his breath coming in big gulps. "I've got to phone HQ. There's been an accident, up above Llyn Gwynant."

"What kind of accident?"

"Car went over the edge." He was still gasping for breath.

"You weren't in it?" There was horror in her voice.

"No. He drove away without me."

"You ran all the way here from Llyn Gwynant?"

"It was quicker than running down to Beddgelert," he said, "and that's where I left my car."

She took his arm. "Come inside," she said. "I'll make you some hot cocoa while you phone." She led him in as if he was one of her students. "You're shivering. Take that wet jacket off," she instructed and came back with a big pink and white towel, which she draped around his shoulders. "The phone's on the kitchen table. Go ahead while I heat up the milk."

She watched him as he talked rapidly into the phone. Water still ran down his face and dripped from his hair onto his shoulders. He looked completely exhausted. Bronwen felt her heart go out to him. She longed to enfold him in her arms, to tell him that everything was going to be alright, but she restricted herself to spooning cocoa into a tall ceramic mug. It was nice to have the chance to look after him for once. She hoped he might also realize how nice it was.

The milk came to a boil and she stirred it into the cocoa. Then she added a generous measure of brandy.

"Here," she said and handed it to him with a smile.

Evan took a sip, then a look of surprise crossed his face. "It's got brandy in it."

"You looked as if you needed it."

"What are you doing, keeping brandy in the house—a respectable schoolteacher like you?"

"Medicinal purposes," she said calmly. "Go on, drink up. Hot liquids are good for shock."

"Thanks. I needed that," he said, taking another sip.

Bronwen appeared again with a basin of warm water and some cotton wool. "Hold still. You've got a nasty cut on your head."

"Have I?" He put his hand up to his temple in surprise. "I was trying to get out of the way of the car. I think I must have hit it on the wall. I didn't notice before." He winced as she sponged it. "Ow, that stings."

"Hold still; you're worse than my infants."

Evan grinned.

"There. Now you look more human," she said. "I couldn't think what it was coming down the hill toward me all covered in mud and gore."

"The Nantgwynant monster." Evan chuckled. "There—now we can start another legend to bring in the tourists."

"Just don't tell poor Evans-the-Meat," Bronwen said. "They don't still think he killed Ted Morgan, do they?"

"We know who killed Ted Morgan now," Evan said. "It was Mr. Dawson, from Beddgelert."

"Dawson, who owns the big hotel? What on earth did he have to do with Ted Morgan?"

"Ted Morgan wrecked his daughter's life. He ran a prostitution racket. Dawson's girl got trapped in it and killed herself."

Bronwen nodded seriously. "I remember hearing about him. He never got over her death, did he?"

"He blamed himself."

Bronwen shivered. "Have they caught him?"

"He just drove his car over a cliff, poor bloke. At least he's out of his torment now."

Bronwen put a hand on Evan's shoulder. "But what did the colonel have to do with it?"

"He didn't kill the colonel," Evan said. "Ted Morgan did. He came here because London had become too hot for him and saw that the colonel was here too. The colonel was one of the regular customers at his girlie club, and we all know that the colonel liked to talk. Ted Morgan couldn't risk the colonel going home and telling everyone where he was. He slipped out of the pub and bashed him over the head. Annie Pigeon saw Ted hurrying back from the riverbank after he'd done it, but she was too scared to say anything."

"Annie Pigeon?" Bronwen asked stiffly.

"Yes, it turns out she was another girl whose life was messed up by Ted Morgan. She came here to get away, only to find him here. It must have been a nightmare for her."

Bronwen gazed thoughtfully out of the window, then she nodded. "So they'll have to release Evans-the-Meat now, won't they?" she asked, deliberately changing the subject.

"In the morning. Although a few nights in jail might have been good for him. It might teach him not to lose his temper so easily."

"I doubt it," Bronwen said. "Would you like more cocoa, or can I warm you up some soup? It's homemade."

Evan got to his feet. "I'd love some, but Sergeant Watkins will be here in a minute."

"You haven't got to go out again?" Bronwen sighed as he went ahead of her to the front door.

"I have to, love." He turned back and looked at her fondly. "It's what a policeman's life is like. It's not all being friendly and helping people. Sometimes we have to handle the not-so-pleasant duties too, and the hours are rotten and so is the pay . . ."

Bronwen nodded. "I understand."

They stood there looking at each other. "I'm sorry I had to break our date tonight," Evan said.

"I thought you were making an excuse because you'd changed your mind," Bronwen answered.

"Why would I change my mind?"

"Because you liked her better."

"Her?" Evan looked genuinely surprised. "You mean Annie Pigeon?"

"You seemed to be spending a lot of time with her. I wondered if you liked the idea of a ready-made family."

Evan shook his head. "I like the idea of my own family some day. About next weekend, Bron . . ." He hesitated. "Is it really important to you to meet your old university friends?"

"Not that important," Bronwen said.

"I was wondering if we could reschedule that date—or better still, make a day of it. We could take a picnic down to the beach and then go on to that Italian restaurant we talked about."

"Now that I think of it," Bronwen said, "those particular friends always were a little too serious for me. I remember they yelled at me once because I walked through a sooty tern's nesting area. How was I to know it was a nesting area? I was trying to take a shortcut to the loo."

Evan laughed. "Oh, Bron," he said. He wrapped his arms around her and held her tightly.

"You're making me all wet!" she complained, laughing too.

"Sorry, I forgot."

"I don't mind," she said, wrapping her arms around his neck before he could let go of her. It seemed very natural when his lips found hers.

Headlights lit the quiet street and a white police car drew to a halt.

"I have to go," Evan said reluctantly releasing her.

"Take care of yourself, Evan," Bronwen said.

"Don't worry about me, I'm indestructible." He started up the path.

"Evan! You've still got a pink towel around your shoulders!" she called after him and ran to exchange it for his jacket.

Sergeant Watkins greeted him with a quizzical smile. "And you were trying to make me believe that you were alone in mortal danger, battling madmen on mountaintops," he joked as Evan got in. "Or was that the hero's welcome home?"

"Something like that, sarge." Evan couldn't resist a big grin as he climbed into the front seat beside Watkins.

211

On Monday morning things were back to normal in Llanfair. Evans-the-Meat opened his shop and started arranging lamb cutlets in the window display. He stuck a sign in them. "Best local Welsh lamb."

Evans-the-Post came out of the post office with a manila envelope in his hand.

"Miss Roberts said I should take this to Mr. Parry Davies straight away," he called to Evans-the-Meat. "She said it's from the university."

Evans-the-Meat came out to look at the envelope. "It will be the official letter from the archaeologists," he said excitedly. "Now we'll find out whether our ruin was really the saint's chapel."

He accompanied Evans-the-Post up the street, calling out to other villagers as they passed. Soon Llanfair looked like Hamlin with Evans-the-Post as pied piper. By the time he reached Chapel Bethel, half the village was in tow.

"This is a great day for Llanfair," the reverend Parry Davies said as he took the envelope and turned it over in his hands.

"Go on, man. Open it. Don't keep us in suspense," Evans-the-Meat exclaimed.

Mr. Parry Davies put on his glasses and opened the envelope. His expression changed as he read down the sheet of paper.

"Well, what does it say?" someone asked. "Isn't it the saint's chapel after all?"

Mr. Parry Davies cleared his throat. " 'We regret to inform you that the ruin we examined last week is nothing more than a former shepherd's hut and sheep byre, not more than one hundred years old.' "

"Not Saint Celert's grave? Not even King Arthur's fort?" Evans-the-Meat asked in stunned disbelief.

Mr. Parry Davies shook his head angrily and crumpled up the letter.

"A good thing, if you ask me," Mrs. Williams muttered to the woman standing next to her. "Now we can go back to being plain old Llanfair again with none of these silly notions."

Evan had been down in Caernarfon all morning, meeting with the D.I. and Sergeant Watkins. One of the things he learned was that Gwyneth Hoskins had called the police while he and Watkins had been in London. She had lost her nerve, apparently, and had to tell them that Sam had been up to Llanfair to see Ted Morgan the night he died. He had accosted Ted after the meeting and asked for a loan. Ted had turned him down. Gwyneth wanted the police to know that she'd been against it all along. She'd never wanted him to go and she'd tried to get him to own up.

"So much for loyalty," Watkins had muttered to Evan. "What a family, eh?"

By the time Evan drove back to Llanfair the excitement about the letter was all over, but he found there was another form of excitement going on. A moving van was parked outside Annie Pigeon's house. Evan hurried over and found Annie coming out with Jenny's Noah's ark lamp in her hand.

"You're going?" Evan asked.

Annie nodded. "That's right. Moving on."

"But why? You're safe now. You don't have to keep running away."

Annie smiled. "This isn't the right place for me. I'd never learn Welsh in a hundred years. If only poor Glynis could have had the chance to come back here, instead of me."

"Where will you go?"

"Back to Manchester to start with. I've got friends there. And then maybe the Lake District. That's pretty too, isn't it, and they speak English there."

"I wish you all the best, Annie," Evan said. "I hope things work out well for you, and Jenny too."

"Thanks to you she won't be growing up in a foster home while her mum is in jail. I expect we'll do just fine."

"Take care of yourself," Evan said.

"You too. Find yourself a nice girl and settle down. You'll make a smashing dad."

"I'll get around to it some time soon, I expect," Evan said.

Across the street at the Red Dragon, Betsy was dusting tables when she noticed the moving van outside Annie's house.

"Harry. Look you here!" she called out excitedly. "She's going!"

"Who is?" Harry came to join her at the window.

"That woman who's been chasing Evan Evans." She glanced thoughtfully up the street. "Now if I could only persuade Bronwen Price to take a teaching job in Antarctica . . ."

214